CHERISHED

Now, holding Nerissa in close embrace, reassurance began to flow through him. Her nearness was a salve to his wounded self-esteem.

He gave her a long, lingering kiss. When he lifted his head to look at her, she was flushed, her eyes bright. She put her arms around his neck, and the sweetness of her kiss went through his veins in a buoyant flood.

"You'll get through this," she whispered. He nodded and kissed her again.

"My sweet Nerissa," he said. Each kiss left him yearning for more.

ARABESQUE 10th ANNIVERSARY
GREAT ROMANCE CONTEST WINNER

Denise Hayes DeLapp

Avid Arabesque Reader and North Carolina Native!

Denise Hayes DeLapp, a school teacher, avid Arabesque romance novel reader, and native of North Carolina, is the winner of the 2004 Great Romance contest.

An only child, DeLapp currently cares for her ailing mother, two very active children, and her husband Reuben at their home outside of Raleigh, North Carolina. DeLapp says that reading Arabesque romance novels is "my addictive leisure-time pleasure." She adds that "with an active family life, I often find myself reading into the early hours of the morning."

DeLapp's own life reads like the pages of an Arabesque novel. She met her husband while visiting friends on a trip to Winston-Salem, North Carolina, and they grew close over a two-year, long-distance relationship. Overcoming obstacles and life's challenges together, they recently celebrated their sixteenth wedding anniversary.

A graduate of Broughton Senior High School and North Carolina Central University, DeLapp has always loved the written word and reads approximately 40 Arabesque novels a year. "It's like a latte that you just *have* to have. Especially my favorite author Rochelle Alers," says DeLapp. "I get consumed with the intense passion that her characters experience!"

Denise Hayes DeLapp will donate the Arabesque books she receives as part of her Grand Prize package to a transitional home for women and Shaw University's tutorial program. "I've enjoyed reading Arabesque novels, and it's a wonderful blessing that I get to pass these uplifting novels along to others in my community," concludes DeLapp.

Arabesque was proud to conduct this nationwide Great Romance contest honoring the avid readers of the Arabesque imprint now celebrating a decade of soulful romance. For a complete list of contest winners, please visit us online at www.BET.com.

CHERISHED

ADRIENNE ELLIS
REEVES

ARABESQUE

BET
BOOKS™

BET Publications, LLC
http://www.bet.com
http://www.arabesquebooks.com

ARABESQUE BOOKS are published by

BET Publications, LLC
c/o BET BOOKS
One BET Plaza
1900 W Place NE
Washington, DC 20018-1211

All Kensington Titles, Imprints, and Distributed Lines are available at special quantity discounts for bulk purchases for sales promotions, premiums, fund-raising, and educational or institutional use. Special book excerpts or customized printings can also be created to fit specific needs. For details, write or phone the office of the Kensington special sales manager: Kensington Publishing Corp., 850 Third Avenue, New York, NY 10022, attn: Special Sales Department, Phone: 1-800-221-2647.

First printing: December 2004
10 9 8 7 6 5 4 3 2 1

Printed in the United States of America

*This book is dedicated to Lauren and Ernest Johnson, Jr.,
and their two sons, Caswell and Ellis, in appreciation for
the many hours we've shared over waffles, books, Folly
Beach, and never-ending, thoughtful conversation.*

ACKNOWLEDGMENTS

Salutations and blessings to my critique group: Nina Bruhns, Kieran Kramer, Vicki Sweatman, Judy Watts, and Stan Yeager.

You've each given me unique insights, the sum total of which is a luminous vision of what it means to strive to be a writer who is honest and true. Memories of our hours together will be forever cherished.

Thank you, dear colleagues.

And always, my loving gratitude to Debbie Reeves for her generous outpouring of time and brilliant computer skills.

Chapter 1

The street curved so gently to the left that Nerissa almost missed it. She'd been staring ahead at the next intersection and debating whether to give up the hunt for today or stay out longer when the sign, TULIP LANE, caught her attention.

It seemed like an omen, she thought, a positive one. She turned into the street, driving slowly so she could examine each house. The tulip, her favorite flower, had long been absent from her life, as had other sources of the kind of beauty that used to give her peace and security.

The brick houses she passed had yards planted with shrubs, flowers, and trees, some more successfully than others. A group of boys lounged around the steps of one house. Two doors down, three small boys played catch while a girl across from them watched longingly.

A nice family street, but she didn't see any vacancies. She should have gone back to the motel.

The ball rolled into the street and a red-haired boy started after it. He stopped to look at her, and when she came to a stop, dashed over to pick it up.

As she waited, Nerissa saw a man almost at the end of Tulip Lane come out of a house and cross the yard to the next house, where he began putting up a sign.

Her heart beat faster. The instant the boy was safely in his yard, she shifted her Toyota pickup in gear and glided past three more houses.

Then she saw it.

There it sat. Her house.

Forlorn, neglected, and misused. It looked exactly like she felt, and it called to her.

One of its four black shutters hung awry. The black paint on the front door was chipped, and the garage door had pictures scrawled on it with colored chalk. The large front yard looked as if it hadn't been cut in weeks. She didn't know what was inside, but the tawny brick structure itself seemed to be of the same solid construction as the other residences.

The man hammered the stake into the ground. He turned the red and white FOR RENT sign forward and looked up as Nerissa stepped from the pickup and started across the yard.

Her nearsightedness had prevented her from seeing the man clearly, although something about his stature had seemed familiar. When she was within speaking distance, she came to an abrupt stop.

The man whose house she had to have was enough like her ex-husband, Ric Cooper, to be his younger brother. The same chocolate-brown coloring, the same square face with wide-set brown eyes that appeared to be so trustworthy, and the same well-shaped mouth that could tell lies with such charm and ease. This man, at several inches above six feet, was taller than Ric and carried more weight, as if he enjoyed his food.

"May I help you?" His voice, deeper than Ric's, jolted her. She couldn't do this. Already the anguish she'd almost buried had begun to stir at just the sight of someone who could be Ric's double. She'd have to try to find another house.

"Are you looking for an address?" A little frown appeared on the man's face.

He must have thought she was crazy standing there as if she'd seen a ghost. She couldn't just walk away.

"How many bedrooms does the house have?" she asked.

"Three bedrooms, two baths," he said slowly.

"It looks like it's been empty a long time." She walked over to the porch, noting several missing bricks on the edges of the steps.

"Only a few months." He laid the hammer on the porch.

As he turned to her, she instinctively took a step back, catching her heel on a chunk of brick and losing her balance.

He reached out to steady her. "Careful," he said, his hand warm and firm around her arm. "Sorry about that. I thought I'd cleared those chunks away." He picked the brick up and laid it beside the hammer.

Her arm tingled from the imprint of his hand. She was right. She couldn't take this house. She'd have to start hunting all over again.

"I'm Bill Denton," he said. "The family who moved out four months ago left the place in terrible condition. I bought it with the intention of attracting a family who would take it as is and make all the repairs in exchange for a lower rent."

In his eyes she saw an assessment that found her

inadequate. She wasn't a man, and it was unlikely that she could put this house in shape.

She lifted her chin. "I'm Nerissa Ramsey. I'd like to see the inside."

That surprised him, she thought as they stared at each other for a moment.

With a slight shrug of his shoulders, he said, "Watch your step," and preceded her across the porch to open the door.

The front room stretched the length of the house. Its three windows faced the street, giving it light. Nerissa saw that the walls were dingy and the rug was dirty. In the three bedrooms, matters got worse.

"How many children lived here?" she asked in the master bedroom, where each wall bore scribbles, small holes, or stains.

"Two small ones and two teenagers. The family was only here for two and a half years. I never came inside so I had no idea the parents let this happen." Hands on hips, Denton shook his head in disgust, his mouth tightened.

"I guess the adults weren't much better," Nerissa said. "This looks like spilled coffee on the rug." If the rest of the place was like this, maybe she would have to back down. Hard work had never bothered her. But how far would her money stretch?

Denton hadn't said how much he wanted. In fact he hadn't opened his mouth. He just led her from room to room until they came to this appalling condition that had forced the disapproving comment.

He might have assumed that his lack of civility would turn her away. Ric had tried that on her, too, she recalled. Denton, however, was nothing to her.

She was the one who'd decide if she wanted the house, regardless of his attitude.

At the end of the hall, they came to a room that was larger than the others. The ivory-paneled walls were set off by dark molding at ceiling level. Sunlight flowing through a pair of French doors made the room glow. Through the glass she saw a concrete patio floor and a spacious fenced-in backyard with healthy shrubs and tall trees.

She couldn't restrain a smile as a freshet of hope quivered deep inside her. Now she knew why this house had called to her. In this sunny, welcoming room she saw exactly where her grandmother's china closet and her own maple hutch would go. Her long dining room table would have the place of honor in the middle of the ample space.

She felt Denton's speculative gaze and knew he'd seen the smile. She didn't care. She'd do whatever was necessary to get this house—short of letting him walk over her.

"This is the family room," Denton said with a slight emphasis on the word 'family' as he gave her a narrowed glance.

She wasn't rising to that. She walked through a wide archway into the kitchen. The usual appurtenances were at one end, all needing a hard scrubbing. At the other, a place for a table in front of three bay windows. Nerissa saw herself filling window boxes with geraniums. She'd eat her meals at the table, watch her flowers grow, and perhaps her bruised heart would begin to heal.

The linoleum was cracked around the refrigerator and

even more so in the adjacent laundry room, where it was peeling off the floor in the corner.

She deliberately stopped and touched it with her toe to see if Denton, as owner, would say anything about it.

"Some water damage there where the washer sat," he said.

"Which means the wood beneath is probably rotted," she said.

Three steps down from the laundry room was the garage, which had been converted into a den. Just the spot for her books. It couldn't be more suitable for what she needed.

The tour ended and by unspoken agreement they walked back into the kitchen and faced each other in front of the windows.

She didn't like him, and he didn't want her to have his house, Nerissa thought. But it was the one she wanted and she intended to have it. She'd seen everything in every room and had a clear picture of the serious task she'd be taking on.

She lifted her chin and fixed her green eyes on his. Now she'd see what excuses this Ric look-alike would present for not wanting her as his tenant.

There was no way this woman could make this house how it should be, Bill thought. He doubted she'd ever known what hard work was.

When he'd grabbed her arm to keep her from falling, he'd felt the silky smoothness of her skin. Plus, she had a way of carrying herself that told him she'd never had to do the physical labor this job required.

She wasn't attractive with her plain features, her hair pulled straight back, and the round glasses perched on her thin nose. She was tall. But her long, loose denim dress hid the legs that might have been the best-looking thing about her, except for her large green eyes that made her light brown skin almost glow. Her eyes made his fingers itch for the camera that usually hung around his neck. None of which mattered because she definitely had some years on him.

Now she faced him, that nose in the air as if she smelled something bad. Any idea he'd had of letting her down easy went up in smoke.

"I guess you can see there's too much here for you to handle, but thanks for stopping by." He took the keys out of his pocket.

"I don't know why you say that, Mr. Denton," she said, those green eyes challenging him.

"This is obviously too much hard, physical labor for a woman." His tone was dismissive.

"That's a very sexist statement, Mr. Denton. Haven't you ever done something that's supposed to be women's work?" Her eyes flashed, and she straightened her back.

Why did he get the impression she was girding herself for battle against an enemy?

"We're not talking about me, Miz Ramsey. All I'm pointing out is that this house will take weeks of cleaning, scraping, scrubbing, painting, making small repairs and getting the yard in shape."

"I understand exactly what's needed, Mr. Denton," she said coolly.

Did she really imagine she could do the enormous job

by herself? But maybe she wasn't by herself. He hadn't thought of that.

"Are you married?" he asked boldly.

"Not anymore," was her calm reply.

Bill could see why, if her husband had had to put up with this tart, unbending female.

He saw a change in her eyes and wondered if his thoughts had shown on his face. Perhaps they had because her voice changed.

"Mr. Denton, let me tell you something about myself. I'm new in Jamison, and I've been looking for the right house for weeks. This is the only one I've seen that I like. I'm fully capable of doing the work you want done, even though I'm a mere woman." Her lips quivered, and the green eyes smiled at him.

She's human after all, he thought, and found himself wondering what it might take to see that smile more often.

"I was a librarian, and now I'm going to open a bookstore here in town. This house has ample space for my books until I can get my business established."

"You were a librarian where?"

"At a tech college in Minneapolis."

"That's a long way from Jamison, South Carolina. You have relatives here?"

"No. A colleague told me about the Charleston area, and I chose Jamison. I like warm weather and I like small towns."

"Any children?"

"No."

He saw the green eyes grow cool again, but he risked one more question.

"So you'd be in the house alone?"

"I'm a grown woman, Mr. Denton. I can take care of myself. What are you asking for rent?"

Bill had a figure in mind for the family man he'd hoped to attract. Maybe he could discourage Miz Ramsey if he upped the price. He named the higher fee and watched her eyes.

He could almost sense the calculations going on in her mind as she glanced out the window. When she turned to him, he knew he'd lost that skirmish.

"Signing a year's lease based on that monthly rent is perfectly acceptable to me," she said.

"You'll excuse me for being blunt, Miz Ramsey, but since you're new in town, I doubt you have any local references."

Let's see her trump that, he thought.

"I made all my financial arrangements in Jamison before I left Minneapolis, Mr. Denton." There was no mistaking the triumphant gleam in her eyes as she drew from her bag a small card and handed it to him.

"This is my bank and you may call them to satisfy yourself that I'm a responsible person."

She'd covered all her bases, and unless he told her flat out he didn't want her next door to him, he'd have to let her have the place.

Then he had an idea. This was the end of September. She was watching him warily when he looked up from the bank card.

"This is what I'll consider, Miz Ramsey," he stated. "A month-to-month lease beginning October first and ending March thirty-first. If at any time in those six months, your work is not up to par, the lease will be terminated."

He meant his voice to clearly say "take it or leave it"

and watched with satisfaction when she blinked and momentarily closed her eyes at this unexpected setback.

He excused the twinge of guilt he felt by telling himself business was business.

She lifted her chin and straightened her back. "I don't think that's necessary, Mr. Denton. But then, you don't know me. I certainly don't know you, but I'll sign the six-month lease with the stipulation that I can have a year's lease if I survive the month-to-month. Do you agree to that?"

"That's the usual procedure," Bill said, wondering how come she was the one now laying down the law.

He knew that despite his twisting and turning, he'd just agreed to six months of trouble.

Chapter 2

This was the best part for Bill.

He had photographed many weddings, beginning when he was a junior in high school. Even then he had an eye that gave his pictures a certain flair.

It had begun when a classmate said his sister was having a small home wedding because they were poor, and she wanted someone to take pictures. He'd told her about Bill, the school paper photographer.

Bill had been excited. Although he'd been experimenting with the camera since receiving it on his ninth birthday, this would be the first chance to document a wedding. The result had been enough pictures to fill several albums. He vowed next time to be more discriminating, but the bride had been delighted. Bill had become the unofficial photographer for his group of friends and contemporaries.

At the University of South Carolina he'd studied photography and psychology. His desire was not only to record the faces he saw in his viewfinder, but to discover the hidden sorrow, joy, weakness, strength, and intelligence that animated those features.

As his skill had developed, his reputation had grown. Now "Denton" on a photograph had a cachet that kept his appointment book filled and his bank account healthy.

This latest wedding had been a traditional affair in a large church. He had shot the prenuptial events—the wedding morning preparations, the ceremony itself, and the family portraits.

Now the sit-down dinner for over one hundred guests was in full swing, and some people were already dancing. Bill roamed the ballroom, his eyes alert for those unique moments that would define this particular wedding and give him the artistic satisfaction he wanted.

In the groom's family, there was a ten-year-old boy whose face stood out with its vitality, humor, and mischievousness. Bill spotted him darting through the crowd to a table where a curly-haired girl was sitting in her wedding finery of an ankle-length white dress tied with a pink satin bow.

Bill would have made book that the boy had just put his tie and jacket back on to impress the girl. He stopped in front of her. On his face determination and uncertainty was etched as he asked her to dance.

Through his camera, Bill saw the boy's tension and the girl's shy delight as she stood and took his hand. One click and Bill knew he had a winner.

Finally the cake was wheeled in, and people crowded around with conversation and laughter. The party was beginning to wind down. From years of experience, Bill knew that the initial excitement and anticipation felt by the newly wedded couple was changing into something new. He shut out the noise and focused all his senses on them.

They cut the cake, his hand over hers. He fed a small

piece to his bride. When she attempted to do the same, Bill saw that her hand was shaking as she looked up at her husband.

He steadied her hand, his face naked with emotion. Ignoring the cake, he drew her to him and kissed her with a tenderness that caught in Bill's throat as he captured the exquisite moment.

He found himself hoping that this would be one of the unions that lasted.

So many didn't. Of all the marriages he'd photographed over the years, he knew at least a fourth of them had dissolved. In his own family the percentage wasn't much better.

One brother and one sister were divorced. Another brother was separated, and his other two sisters seemed married to their careers.

"I don't know where we went wrong, your Dad and I," his mother often complained. "Six grown children and only two grandchildren."

His parents had been married fifty-five years and still thought they were lucky to have found each other.

After the wedding Bill prepared a late supper—grilled potato strips, tender asparagus, thick tomato slices, and lastly, salmon steak with Cajun seasoning.

His friends laughed when he said that getting every aspect of a dish in perfect balance was akin to composing a picture. It didn't always work, but it was always his goal.

Just as his dinner was ready, the phone rang.

"This is Nerissa Ramsey, Mr. Denton."

"Is there something the matter?"

"Nothing at all. We haven't done the contract yet, and I

don't have the keys to the house yet, but I intend to start on the yard tomorrow. Do you have any objections?"

Her tone of voice implied that she would demolish any reasons he might have.

"It's supposed to rain tomorrow, Miz Ramsey." He was equally stiff.

"Do you have any objections, Mr. Denton?" she repeated as if he hadn't spoken.

"No."

"Then may I borrow a rake?"

Borrow his rake? He'd intended to rake his own yard tomorrow. If it didn't rain. Still, anything to get her out of his hair.

"Yes," he said,

"Thank you, Mr. Denton."

That woman has some nerve, he fumed. How's she going to do all the work that yard requires if she has to borrow a rake from me?

Hoping his food wasn't cold, he set his plate on the table, added sourdough bread with garlic butter, and started the coffee to brew. He ate slowly, savoring each bite while listening to a quiet sonata as an antidote to the music and chatter that had assaulted him these past hours.

He couldn't get the image of that kiss, with all it implied, out of his mind. It reminded him of when his best friend, Chris Shealy, had married Magnolia Rose Sanders. When the minister said, "I now pronounce you husband and wife," Chris had looked as if paradise had opened before him.

Chris and Magnolia had gone through hard times before arriving at the acceptance of their love. Bill knew today's couple had also overcome difficulties.

Maybe that was what it took to generate the intensity of emotion he'd witnessed.

He had a fleeting idea that if Miz Nerissa Ramsey had received such a look of promise on her wedding day, she would not be divorced. It was no wonder she'd become so bitter.

He took his coffee out on the deck. Perhaps the cool night air would clear his head and he could think of something besides weddings.

The wind had picked up, causing a stir in the trees. Soon he'd have to do something about the fallen leaves that were getting to be a problem. The sickle moon rode the sky, and he speculated about what it must be like to be an astronaut in that limitless space so far away from earth and home.

Would he feel as lonely there as he did here?

Where did that come from? Was he truly lonely or was this the backwash of thinking too much about weddings and marriage?

He had to admit that the attraction of dating lovely girls when he and Chris had played the field together had begun to dim at about the time Chris and Magnolia Rose became serious.

Since their wedding, the steady increase in his work had given him a good excuse to refuse the social invitations he used to enjoy.

Except where Nancy Fisher was concerned.

She was one of their high school crowd who now worked as a caterer. They'd formed a pleasant relationship, often cooking and eating together. Lately it seemed to Bill their dating might be drifting in a more serious direction.

One more cup of coffee, then he'd call it a night. He

was tired of his unprofitable thoughts. As he settled back with his cup, the phone beside him rang. He automatically noted it was ten-thirty as he said, "Hello." Perhaps it was Nancy.

"This is Nerissa Ramsey, Mr. Denton. Is it too late to call?"

"What is it this time, Miz Ramsey?" Didn't the woman ever go to bed?

"I'm going to need an edger tomorrow too. May I borrow yours, please?"

"Are you sure that's all?" He couldn't help his sarcastic tone.

"That's all. Thanks."

"Go to bed, Miz Ramsey, so we can both get some sleep."

Chapter 3

Nerissa was in her element.

Clad in her favorite working outfit of shapeless cords, loose checked shirt, and red headwrap, she raked the first layer of leaves in what she already thought of as her backyard.

She started in the far right corner, which held a small slide and swing. When she shook them, they were firm and steady. Some lucky parents had installed them and watched their young children go gleefully down the slide and pump their legs in the swing.

She wished she could have been such a parent, but that joy had been denied her.

She raked more energetically and after an hour had a very large pile. It was break time. The predicted rain had not appeared, but the air was humid. She should've worn a tank top and shorts. Seating herself on the steps outside the French doors, she poured some coffee from the thermos. Hot weather or cold, it was her usual restorative.

She'd arrived at seven prepared to knock on Denton's door if necessary but decided to check the back first. It was good she did because the yard tools were there, leaning against the fence. He must have put them out early this morning. Or maybe last night. He'd probably been annoyed by her late calls, but he'd get over it.

After all, he was the one who'd insisted on that crazy month-to-month lease, putting unnecessary pressure on her. Treating her as if she were some irresponsible fly-by-night even after she'd given him her financial bona fides.

She'd show him that no matter what he did, she'd outwit him. Her first proof would be this backyard. She finished her coffee and went back to work. Her experienced eye told her that the layers of matted leaves meant the yard had been neglected for several seasons. Branches and twigs lay thick under the trees.

As she worked, she studied the layout, picturing what she would plant once the place was cleared. Azaleas, for sure, against the back fence. In as many colors as she could find.

Muscles she hadn't used since selling the house she and Ric had owned began to complain, but she might as well get used to it. She knew she had days of this back-breaking toil ahead. Who would take on such a task unless he or she wanted the house and intended to stay? That was why Denton's implication of her irresponsibility made her mad.

She'd taken her third load of debris to the front curb when Denton strolled through her gate. In his brown slacks, pristine white sports shirt, and brown sandals, he looked crisp, cool, and unhurriedly sexy. That figured.

She was crumpled, sweaty, and rushed. He was the last person she wanted to see. She straightened her back, tilted her chin, and looked him in the eye.

"Good afternoon, Mr. Denton. Thanks for the tools."

"You're welcome," he said as he surveyed the yard, hands in his pockets. "You've certainly put them to good use. I can't believe how much you've already done."

Pleasantly surprised that he could be complimentary, Nerissa was about to say something appreciative when he spoiled it.

"Why didn't you use my wheelbarrow for the leaves instead of that tarp?"

"I didn't have the wheelbarrow." Surely that was obvious.

His dark glance held hers. "You didn't have any problem last night asking for what you needed, Miz Ramsey. You could have asked for the wheelbarrow this morning."

"I had the tarp in my pickup. It works." Why didn't he go back to whatever he'd been doing and let her get on with this grubby job?

He shrugged, but she saw a gleam in his eye. "I came to tell you I have the contract. We can go over it now if you like. Or maybe you'd rather wait until tomorrow."

Tomorrow when she could be as clean and refreshed as he was? She'd love that, but he'd have to take her as she was right now. Smudges and all. Too bad if he didn't like it. She wanted the keys to her house.

"I'm ready now, Mr. Denton," she said, and laid the rake on the tarp. "I just need to wash my hands."

They entered his house through a spacious deck that was screened and comfortably filled with the kind of lounge furniture she liked. She followed him through his kitchen and den.

"The bathroom is the first door on the left in the hall," he said.

She looked even worse than she'd imagined, and for

a brief moment she thought of returning tomorrow, freshly showered and appropriately attired. No. She wouldn't give in to vanity. Denton wasn't someone she wanted to impress. Her brain was working regardless of how she looked.

Minutes later, washed and cool, she felt ready to take on the negotiations. When she left the bathroom, she saw that the hall was a gallery of sorts, exhibiting black-and-white photographs. She was drawn to a family portrait of mother, father, and baby. Instead of sitting stiffly in chairs, they were standing in a relaxed pose, his arm around her, she leaning into him while holding the baby. Love, pride, and tenderness shone in their faces. In the corner was the name Denton.

He took that picture? Swiftly she glanced at a few more. All by him. How could the man about to make her sign an unfair lease take a picture that made her heart ache?

He was waiting for her in the kitchen. "If you don't mind, we'll sit in here," he said as he pulled back a chair for her at the round oak table.

An icy pitcher of lemonade and two filled glasses were on the table. The first long drink felt good going down her throat.

He sat across from her and opened a folder. "This is the standard rental agreement," he said, handing her a copy. "As you can see, the first paragraph names the landlord, tenant, address of the property, and the rental amount, beginning October first and ending March thirty-first. Then we come to the security deposit."

Nerissa looked at him. "That's to ensure that the

property is left as the tenant found it. It's not applicable in this case."

"I was about to point that out," he said stiffly.

"It says I can't have pets without your written consent. Suppose I want a dog or cat?" Ric had been afraid of dogs, and pets were not allowed in her apartment in Minneapolis. Now was her chance to have one.

"I've no objection as long as you're responsible for its behavior and any damage it does. You have a pet?" His brown eyes widened with curiosity.

"Not yet, but I intend to get a dog."

"What kind?"

"A Lab if I can find one."

He nodded approvingly. "They're good dogs. I had one when I was a kid. Raised him from a puppy."

He looked nostalgic, and for a moment there was agreement between them.

The paragraphs on insurance, pest control and subletting passed without comment. It was the next item that had Nerissa preparing to do battle if necessary.

"It says, Mr. Denton, that you're to make repairs to keep the premises in a fit and habitable condition for the tenant." She laid the paper down and faced him. "What exactly does that include?"

"If the place caught on fire or was damaged by the weather, I'd be responsible for making it fit to live in again." He looked up at her from beneath raised eyebrows.

"I'm not concerned about what might happen. I want to know about the floors as they are now. We both saw how dirty the rugs are in every room. They make the premises unfit, Mr. Denton."

He pushed his papers aside and sat back in his chair. She felt he was giving her his whole attention for the first time and it made her self-conscious and at the same time slightly flustered. She wondered what he was thinking about her.

"Carpet shampoo machines are plentiful here. I don't know if you had them in Minneapolis, Miz Ramsey, but you can rent them from most grocery stores." He spoke softly, his eyes locked with hers.

Indignation rose in her like a geyser. She hated using those heavy machines and they certainly weren't efficient enough to restore the carpets she'd seen yesterday. But that wasn't the issue. The landlord was supposed to take care of the flooring. Not the tenant.

She could see in his eyes that he expected an explosion from her. Instead she spoke calmly. "I believe Minneapolis has such machines, Mr. Denton. However, they do not interest me, there or here, since this is clearly your responsibility."

"I pointed out to you yesterday that putting this house in shape required too much hard physical labor for a woman. Are you telling me you can't clean the carpeting?" His voice was still silky soft, but his eyes were steely.

Nerissa refused to be intimidated. "That isn't what I'm telling you, Mr. Denton. I am simply pointing out that it is the responsibility of the landlord to provide decent floor covering for the tenant. While we're on the subject, that would also include the rotted place in the laundry room."

She watched his eyes. Was he truly incensed or was he playing a cat-and-mouse game with her? She couldn't back down because she knew she was right. On the other hand, she did want the house.

"Perhaps, Mr. Denton, we should consider a compromise," she offered.

"Such as what?" The wariness in his voice was unmistakable.

"I'd be willing to take care of the flooring so you wouldn't be bothered. The cost, of course, would have to be deducted from my rent. I'd give you all the receipts so you could be sure I wasn't cheating you."

If Denton went for this, he'd be worse than Ric, who had often tried to weasel out of an unarguable responsibility.

"That's the silliest compromise I ever heard!" His voice rose sharply as he thrust his face forward. "Did you really think I'd fall for that?"

Her voice rose also as she leaned across the table, agreeableness forgotten and green eyes blazing.

"You asked for it!"

Suddenly her eyes shifted to something behind him. Denton turned around.

A petite young woman with long hair, impeccably dressed in heels and an ivory knit dress, could be clearly seen through the screen door.

"I knocked, but I guess you didn't hear me, Bill," she said. "Am I interrupting something?"

Chapter 4

No man wants to deal with two women at the same time. Especially when he was dating one and the other prickled his nerves every time he saw her.

Finesse! That was what the situation called for. No one could accuse Bill Denton of lacking in that department. He came smoothly to his feet. "Excuse me, please," he said to Nerissa and went to open the door for Nancy Fisher.

"Hi, Nancy, come on in." Her perfume drifted through the air as she walked by him, and she wasn't wearing her usual casual clothes. Must be on her way to some event in her knit dress and heels.

He hadn't expected her to drop by, but now that she was here she could meet his new tenant. Assuming that Miss High-and-Mighty Ramsey agreed to rent his house.

"Nerissa Ramsey, this is Nancy Fisher," he said.

"Hello, Miss Fisher," Nerissa said formally.

"Nice to meet you, Miss Ramsey." Nancy looked at the papers on the table. "I can come back if you're busy, Bill."

"We're going over a rental contract for the house next

door, but we can finish it another time. If that's all right with you, Miz Ramsey?" he said courteously.

"Of course, Mr. Denton." She gathered her papers as he stood. "Good-bye, Miss Fisher," she said and, head held high, left the kitchen.

Bill had to move fast to open the screen door for her. Their eyes met, and the look she gave him made him wonder how successful his finesse had been.

"Have a seat, Nancy, or would you rather sit in the den?" She'd been in his house many times but seemed to be uncomfortable.

"This is okay," she said, but instead of sitting, she went to the window. Bill joined her and they watched Nerissa go into the yard next door.

"What happened to the family man who'd rehabilitate your house for a lowered rent?" Nancy asked.

Bill felt slightly defensive. "She's moved here from Minneapolis and has been looking for the right place. Said this was the house she wanted and was willing to do all the work." He watched as Nerissa attacked the leaves again.

"Is there a husband or children?" Nancy raised her eyebrows at him.

"She said neither one."

"Three bedrooms, two baths, and an enclosed garage, as I recall. Right?"

"Right."

Nancy looked at him with open astonishment. "Aren't you being unfair to let this older woman take on all that work? How do you know she can do it?"

Bill definitely felt defensive now. "She assured me that she can and will do what is necessary. That's what we were doing when you arrived. Working out the details. It's just a straight business deal, Nancy."

"I hope you know what you're doing," she said, turning away from the window.

Amen to that, he thought. "What can I get you to drink? Lemonade, coffee, ginger ale, tea, water?"

"Nothing, Bill." She was fidgeting at the counter, her back to him. "I always liked this ceramic bowl. It's so decorative."

Bill gently turned her around and kept his hands on her shoulders. Her soft brown eyes avoided his.

"What's the matter, Nan? I know I haven't called you lately, but I had to do several weddings and a family portrait. How about dinner and a movie now?" he said persuasively.

"No, Bill. No more dinners or movies." She moved from under his hands and put some space between them.

"Why?" He leaned back against the counter.

"I want us to go back to just being friends." Now her eyes met his.

"Well, of course. We always were." What was she getting at? They'd been part of the same crowd that had hung out together from high school days on.

"That's my point. It's never going to be anything else." She picked up the small ceramic bowl and turned it in her hands. "No matter how often we have dinner and go to movies together."

"Why not? What'd I do?" His lips tightened.

"You've done nothing, Bill. That's what I'm talking about." Her eyes were no longer soft.

His voice rose and took on an edge. "Exactly what'd you want me to do?"

"It's not a matter of what I wanted you to do. It's what you didn't want to do." Her eyes flashed and she clutched the bowl.

Bill looked at her in frustration. "I don't get it," he said, jamming his hands in his pockets.

"Let me explain it to you in simple phrases." She set the bowl on the counter. "You and Chris Shealy have been best friends and running buddies forever. Then he married Maggie Rose. That left you alone. I was around, so you latched on to me."

"Stop right there. I didn't force you to go out with me," he said hotly.

"I liked being with you."

"Then what is the problem?" He articulated each word.

"The relationship, if that's what we have, isn't going anywhere because you don't want it to."

The simple statement had a firm emphasis that Bill felt as she kept her eyes on his.

It knocked him back for a second. "You don't know that!" He came away from the counter and glared at her.

"You're wrong, Bill. I do know," she said quietly.

"Maybe you're the one who doesn't want it to go further," he retorted.

The disappointed look she gave him reminded Bill of when his mother used to catch him in a sorry excuse for something he'd done.

"I can't keep waiting for you to make up your mind." She took a breath. "I've met a man I like, and it's definitely mutual. He has no problem letting me know how he feels. So this is good-bye for you and me. Except as old school friends. Find someone you can fall in love with, Bill."

She turned quickly and was gone before he recovered from his shock.

He rubbed his hands over his face. Maybe he shouldn't have gotten up this morning. In the last half hour, two women had walked out that door after laying his soul to rest.

What he needed was a strong drink. He opened the refrigerator and took out his one hundred percent Colombian coffee. He added an extra measure to the drip pot and in a few minutes it was ready.

He poured some into his ten-ounce mug, adding sugar and cream. He took that first long taste. It was satisfying. Soothing. Comforting. Totally unlike women. He settled in a deck chair and took another swallow.

What had gotten into Nancy? Everything was fine as far as he was concerned. In fact, he'd had the idea they were getting closer from little things she'd said. So where'd she get off wanting him to make up his mind? She was free and he was free, so what was the hurry? He saw her when it was convenient. Or when he'd been alone too long in his studio. She'd never objected before.

It probably wasn't him at all, or anything he'd done. Now that he thought about it, he could see it wasn't his fault, no matter what she said. No woman, including Nancy, had ever dumped him. Nancy had met some hotshot who'd probably come on to her pretty strong. She'd felt guilty about seeing both him and this new guy, so she'd planned that little scene in the kitchen.

If that was what she wanted, it was all right with him. He wished her luck. Sooner or later he'd meet Hotshot and see how well they fit.

He took his empty mug to the sink and washed it out. He went into the studio and began the serious business of selecting the best pictures for the wedding album he was working on.

He was looking at the women with hands outstretched to catch the bridal bouquet. The colors were sharp, their faces gay. It was a keeper, so he put it on that pile. The next one, taken from a slightly different angle, showed one of the bridesmaids, her arms barely lifted, with her face turned away, her gaze fixed on someone beyond the camera's eye. That was the keeper, not the other. As he placed it on the pile, his studio cordless phone rang.

"Denton's," he said.

"Are you the man who takes the pictures?" a young girl's voice asked.

"Yes, I am. What can I do for you?" he asked curiously.

"I want a picture of me and my little sister," she said softly.

"How old are you?" Kids didn't call about pictures. Their parents did.

"I'm nine and my sister's six."

"May I talk to your mom or your dad about this?"

"Oh, no, it's a surprise for their anniversary. That's why I'm calling you." She hurried on. "I know you take pictures of kids. I saw some at my cousin's house."

"What's your cousin's name?"

"Annamae Peebles. You remember her?"

"Yes, I do." The Peebles' daughter had graduated with highest honors, and he'd taken pictures of the celebration. "What's your name?"

"Breia Peebles. My sister's Josie. I've been saving, and now I've got almost twenty dollars because I got ten from my aunt for my birthday. Will that be enough?" she asked.

A Denton photograph hadn't cost twenty dollars since Bill had been in college, but he had a soft spot for kids like Breia who only wanted to do something nice for her parents.

When he got through talking with her, they'd arranged that her older cousin would bring them over on Friday. He put it in his appointment book for the afternoon. Breia couldn't be certain of the time, she'd said, but her cousin would call.

As he resumed his task, he recalled the Peebles family. The genes of their African ancestors were still strong, and he'd enjoyed the challenge of highlighting those details in each face. Maybe Breia and Josie had them too.

Two hours later, Bill was glad to stand up when the front door chimes rang. He was surprised to see Nerissa Ramsey there.

He blinked at her for a second, then opened the door. "Come in." The lease. That was what she'd come for. He'd successfully distanced himself from their earlier encounter by spending time in his studio.

"Can we finish the lease, Mr. Denton?" She held her copy in her hand.

"Have a seat while I get my copy." His front room had a sofa, three cushy chairs, and one with a straight back. He bet that the straight-backed chair was the one she'd choose.

When he returned, she was in the wine-red cushy chair, her legs stretched out. Long legs that went on and on. He blinked again.

She must be tired. He would be if he'd raked the yard all day. Tired or no, he wasn't going to permit any more nonsense about the flooring. He'd control the rest of the discussion and get her out of his hair. He jumped in as if they'd never talked about that part.

"I'll take care of the flooring. Purchasing the carpeting and having it installed throughout the house will take some time. I'll make the arrangements tomorrow, but I can't say what their schedule will be."

He saw a flicker of uncertainty in her eyes. "Do you have any idea of how long it might take?"

"Anywhere from five days to three weeks from what I hear. Depends on how backed up their installers are."

"I see."

Something was going on behind those intelligent eyes, but he hurried on before she could come up with one of her weird ideas.

He went over returned checks, late charges, and required notices. It was only when they came to the paragraph about the landlord having the right to enter the dwelling to examine it that she seemed to come to life.

Her head shot up. "You can come in anytime?"

"If you read on, you'll see I'd have to give you twenty-four hours notice. Except for emergencies."

That was the last item. He waited to see what she was going to do. Put up with the things that irritated her and do all that back-breaking work just because the house had caught her fancy? Or be sensible and acknowledge that this was not the right proposition for her and save them both a lot of unnecessary trouble?

"I'm ready to sign the lease, Mr. Denton." There was no hint of uncertainty in her voice or in the glance she leveled at him. "May I borrow your pen, please?"

He watched her sign and wondered if she'd ever been

in the military. If not, they'd lost a good recruit because she sure didn't back down from difficult situations. He couldn't help feeling a grudging admiration.

She took a check from her pocket and passed it to him with the lease. Her handwriting was like her, bold and assertive.

"I didn't expect the rent until Tuesday," he said.

"Tomorrow I'm going to get a phone and have the utilities put in my name. I want to start some inside cleaning." She stood up. "I need my keys, please."

For a wild moment Bill was tempted to say she'd have to wait until he had them made. Just for the pleasure of annoying her and setting off sparks in those green eyes of hers.

"Thank you, Mr. Denton," she said as he put the keys in her hand.

She clutched them as if they were precious. When she looked up, he saw lines of strain around her mouth and eyes relax. It made him want to see her totally relaxed and smiling. Bet it'd take some years off her.

"Now that you're officially my tenant, I need to know how to get in touch with you. What's your telephone number?" His pen was poised over the lease.

"I'll let you know as soon as I get it tomorrow."

She'd misunderstood. "I mean where you're staying now," he explained.

"I'll only be there one more night," she said.

Maybe she didn't like that motel. "Where're you moving to?"

She looked at him strangely. "To my house, Mr. Denton. The one I just paid you for."

The woman was crazy. "But the house is dirty and very empty. Or had you forgotten?"

"I haven't forgotten. I'm not wasting my money paying the motel every night when I have this nice big house," she said. "That doesn't make any sense."

"You can't move into a house that hasn't a stick of furniture in it, Nerissa!"

In his agitation, he'd used her first name.

"Watch me!" she said.

Chapter 5

Today is the first day of the rest of your life.

Nerissa had often seen that slogan and dismissed it as being as fanciful as a snowflake retaining its shape on a hot August day.

However, as she unlocked the door of the house at 200 Tulip Lane, she felt she'd crossed the threshold of a new phase in her life.

Her divorce had ended a drama that had begun when she'd met Ric Cooper at a library conference in Minneapolis. They'd shared a passion for finding black writers who wrote well but had been overlooked. They liked skating in the winter, long walks, thoughtful movies, and jazz.

When Ric proposed marriage, Nerissa had been certain her fairy godmother had made all her wishes come true. The first year had been idyllic, the second less so, as Nerissa yearned for children but Ric said he wasn't ready yet. By the end of the third year, he still wasn't ready to start a family and she realized the marriage was in serious trouble. But her vows kept her hoping and trying to make it work.

In the middle of the fourth year, a graduate student

had come to see Nerissa with the news that she was six
months pregnant with Ric's child.

That same day Nerissa threw all of Ric's belongings
in the yard, changed the locks, and talked to her lawyer.
It was the end of that era in her life.

Today was different. As she walked through the
house, empty of furnishings but filled with sunlight, a
sense of welcome and rightness enveloped her.

She was certain the strength and determination that
had carried her through her mother's death when she
was eighteen, leaving her to help her dad with her two
younger sisters, and through the failure of her marriage
when she was thirty-five would revivify her future now
that she'd turned thirty-nine.

She didn't care what obstacles arose. She'd overcome
them and transform this place, then establish her book
boutique.

She'd had the utilities turned on. Now she needed to
locate the telephone connections so she could buy
phones. She found three and left the house. Denton's
Mercedes wasn't in the driveway. She hoped he was out
keeping his promise about the carpeting.

When she returned, her pickup was piled high with
linens, blankets, a plastic tub of housewares, cleaning
materials, and yard tools—all from her storage unit.
There was also a rental cot as well as her luggage from
the motel. Now she could really get down to business.

Opening the garage door, she stored everything in the
space which she now considered her den and which
she'd decided to use as living quarters until her furniture
could be moved in.

Meanwhile, the defaced garage door offended her.

Children's scrawls were fine in their place, but not where she had to see them every time she drove up. The loose shutter was the other thing that had to be corrected at once. It made the house look trashy.

As she moved closer to see if she could fix it herself, an envelope stuck in the front door caught her eye. She ran lightly up the steps to get it.

Her name was printed in bold letters on the front of the sealed letter. It had to be from Denton. No one else around here knew her. She took out the single sheet and read:

> *Nerissa, I've ordered the carpet. They said it should be in the store by Thursday. The installers can begin on Friday but won't be able to finish until the middle of next week. Tried to push them, but that's the best I could do. Will be back on Wednesday from Columbia. Bill Denton*

He'd kept his word. She'd give him a brownie point for that. He said he'd be away until Wednesday. How much could she get done here in the front to make his eyes open when he returned? Maybe everything, if she could find someone to fix the shutter.

After a quick trip to the nearest home-fixit store, the garage door gleamed with a new coat of paint. She sat on the porch steps to take a breather. Her head itched under her red work scarf, and she bent her neck to untie the knot. As she whipped the fabric off and ran her fingers through her soft curls, a tall woman in jeans and a T-shirt strolled up.

"I saw you painting that garage, and I had to come tell

you how glad I am to see it clean again." The brown eyes in the long face were friendly. "I'm Pearline Rogers, and I live two doors down across the street." She pointed at a white frame house with dark blue shutters.

Nerissa said her name and invited Pearline to sit. "I thought to get the crayon off with some kind of cleaner, but the man at the store said that wouldn't work. It was simpler to paint over it."

"Those kids were nice when you talked to them. So were the parents. They just didn't seem to know how to take care of anything," Pearline said. "You from around here, Nerissa?"

Pearline's curiosity, kindly and unguarded, was what Nerissa had grown used to since coming to Jamison. "I've just moved here from Minneapolis," she said, returning her visitor's frank gaze.

"I've never been to Minneapolis, but I hear it gets really cold there."

Nerissa nodded. "Lots of snow and ice in the winter."

"You've come to the right place. It never gets what you'd call cold in this part of the state. You have family?"

"Not here. Just me."

It'd be nice if she could say differently, but after the divorce she'd isolated herself by finding an apartment in another part of Minneapolis. Too unhappy for a social life, she'd made no new friends. Her sisters and dad had urged her to join them in Seattle. She'd accepted their invitation with several visits but felt smothered by their sympathy.

The opportunity to leave Minneapolis came when she'd been vested in the library system for fifteen years. With that money and her share of the sale of the house she'd shared with Ric, she'd arrived in Jamison where there was no past to confront her.

She wanted to know this new neighborhood, and since Pearline was asking questions, she'd ask some too.

"You have family, Pearline?"

"Harold, that's my husband, and I have four grown children scattered all over the place. There's six grands, too. I'll show you their pictures when you come over."

Anticipating the next question, Nerissa volunteered information. "I used to be married, but there were no children."

"There's plenty on this street. Last count there were ten."

"I've seen the young children playing ball." Nerissa pointed to her left. "Near the end of the block there's a house where teenage boys seem to meet."

"That's the Russell family," Pearline said. "Ross, their oldest, cuts grass. You aren't thinking of doing all this lawn yourself, are you?" She made an expansive gesture toward the wide yard.

"I thought . . ." Nerissa began, but Pearline steamrolled right over her.

"Because you don't have to do it. He'll do it for you. Their number's in the book."

"Thanks," Nerissa said when Pearline drew a breath. Maybe this loquacious neighbor knew someone who could fix the shutter. She barely got the words out of her mouth when Harold was volunteered.

"He fixed ours and he'd be happy to fix yours. I'll send him over."

"I don't want to put your husband to any trouble."

"It's no trouble. He likes to do stuff around the

house. When you come over, he'll show you the work-shop he made."

Nerissa heard Pearline's second reference to coming over. If she wanted to be a part of this neighborhood, she'd have to get used to such casual visiting.

"You've got a real good landlord, you know," Pearline said.

The change of subject took Nerissa by surprise. "He seems nice," she replied with tongue firmly in cheek. "Have you known him long?"

"All his life." Pearline shifted to a more comfortable position as she faced Nerissa. "Him and our second son, Kenny, that's thirty-four now, were in the same grade all through school. Bill's from a nice family. We used to live in the same neighborhood. We moved over here twelve years ago, and when Bill came, we teased him about wanting to be close to us."

So that was Denton's age! Five years her junior. Why wasn't he married? He was attractive, intelligent, and had a good career. Maybe he had been or was about to be engaged to Nancy Fisher, although yesterday she hadn't sensed a strong emotional tie between them. She was reluctant to ask Pearline about him. As it turned out, she didn't need to.

"Harold and I tell Bill he's being left behind. Most of his friends are married." She lowered her voice to confidential tones, even though there was no one in sight. "I thought it'd be him and Nancy Fisher, espe-cially after his best friend, Chris Shealy, had his big wedding two years ago." She shook her head. "I don't know what he's waiting for. I told his mother I think he's hard to please." She paused to wave at someone in a passing car.

Nerissa could well believe that Denton was choosy. It went with the arrogance she'd seen in him, but she couldn't say that to Pearline.

"Maybe he's too busy with his career," she said.

"He's busy all right. Goes all over with his camera. He's won a lot of awards, and we're all so proud of him." She looked at Denton's house, then turned back to Nerissa. "Harold says he just hasn't met the right woman."

Nerissa couldn't find an answer to that, and it was time to get back to work. She looked at her watch, hoping Pearline would notice.

"I've sat here long enough," Pearline said, and repeated her promise to send Harold to fix the shutter. She dismissed Nerissa's thanks with "That's what neighbors do."

Later that day, Nerissa used her big clippers to trim the shrubs while the Russell boy mowed the lawn. Inside the house, she cleaned everything in the kitchen and bathroom, then ate a large bowl of her favorite cream of mushroom soup, took a hot shower and, exhausted, fell into her hastily made-up cot.

Another hot shower in the morning at six took away the lingering stiffness. Two cups of strong coffee and a toasted bagel gave her sufficient energy to begin painting the bedrooms.

She wondered what Pearline thought about Denton renting the house to her instead of to a family man. There was no doubt that she and Harold knew all about it. With all of her questions and talkativeness, Pearline had not brought it up. That meant she could be tactful when she thought it was called for. So why had she told Nerissa her concern about Denton getting married?

She pondered this as she painted a line beneath the ceiling in the second bedroom. Distracted, she leaned to catch the corner and the ladder moved. Panicked, she steadied it while she held her breath, then came down and sat on the floor. Her heart thudded in her chest.

All she could think of was how Denton would react if she fell or spilled paint all over the floor. Even if he didn't say anything, which was highly unlikely, his expressive eyes would register his feelings. He'd help her up and say something sympathetic, but inside he'd be thinking that he knew all along this was too much for her.

It wasn't too much. Wait till he came back and saw the front of the house looking as good as his. Then she'd show him the kitchen and the bedrooms. The two smaller ones were almost done. She'd already spackled the holes in the master bedroom. Only one coat of the high-quality paint was needed, and her long-handled roller made short work of the walls.

If that didn't impress him, she didn't know what would.

Bill had intended to leave Columbia earlier, but his host at the college had insisted on a late lunch, which stretched to well over an hour, delaying Bill's trip to the city's main library to do some research.

Every year he gave workshops at the college on photography. This year the students had been very attentive and asked good questions. One young woman said she intended to make independent movies. This had led to such an animated discussion of black filmmakers that Bill had to cut it short.

He grinned at the memory of the quiet boy with sleepy eyes who'd not said a word until almost the end of the period. Then he'd asked a highly technical question about the difference between certain characteristics of a Canon and a Nikon camera.

Bill could've spent at least another hour on the answer. Instead he put the information in a few succinct sentences, ending with reference materials the boy could read.

Such challenges were good. Stimulating. Kept you on your toes. That kid might have deliberately waited until the last minute to put Bill on the spot.

Like Nerissa. Nearly every word she said came out as a challenge. Was she like that with everyone? She'd been what? A librarian. They were supposed to entice people to read, so he couldn't see her acting with others the way she did with him. And now she was going to open a bookstore. She'd never attract customers with that snobbish, offputting attitude she gave him.

So maybe it was just him. For some reason he rubbed her the wrong way.

He suddenly braked as three huge trucks in front of him moved over to exit at the scales. Bill watched for an opening, slid into the fast lane, and put his mind on getting to Jamison.

It was dusk when he arrived. His headlights illuminated his next-door property as he turned into his driveway. He got out of his car, walked over to Nerissa's driveway, and stared.

How did she get the lawn mowed, the shrubs trimmed,

the shutter straightened, and the garage door painted so fast?

He could wait until morning, but he wanted to know now. Nerissa answered his ring with a paintbrush in her hand. She wore her red handkerchief, tight jeans, and a thin red top with streaks of paint on it.

Her face looked a little flushed as she held the door open.

"Mr. Denton. Come in."

"You might as well call me Bill because I'm calling you Nerissa," he said, holding her gaze.

As he stepped across the threshold, she moved and narrowly missed swiping his jacket with paint.

"Careful!" he exclaimed, grasping her wrist.

He watched, fascinated, as she caught her bottom lip with her even white teeth, and the flush he'd suspected deepened into a subtle rose. Her green eyes met his.

"I'm sorry," she said softly, then looked at his fingers still holding her wrist.

"It's okay," he said, following her gaze. Her skin was warm and smooth.

He had the oddest notion that instead of releasing her, he should pull her toward him. Instantly he let her go and jammed his hands in his pockets.

Say what he had to say and leave.

"I just drove up and saw the front. I don't know how you got all that done so quickly, but it looks very good." He looked at the wall opposite him that was already painted. "And now you've started in here. You really do work fast."

"Thanks." She laid the brush across the can of paint. "Let me show you something else."

He followed her down the hall, trying not to notice her leggy, sexy walk.

When she showed him the two smaller bedrooms, he was surprised. The finished master left him almost speechless.

"When did you do all this painting?"

"Today." A smug little smile played around her lips as her eyes challenged him.

She showed him the bathroom and the kitchen, both of them immaculate. "This is what I did last night."

The woman was a marvel, but he wasn't going to tell her that. He could see she was already gloating. Her smug smile gave her away.

"Did you get any sleep at all?"

"Enough," she said, her arms folded.

"Speaking of which, where did you sleep?" he demanded.

Without a word she led him to the den. It, too, was clean but sparsely furnished with a narrow cot, a table, several chairs, and a large table lamp. She'd hung a dark blue curtain at the window.

"You comfortable here?" There must be something he could find fault with.

"Yes, I am." The smugness was replaced with surprise.

Back in the front room, he said, "You got my note about the carpet?"

"I did. The walls need to be done before the carpet's laid. That's why I'm doing them now."

Hands in pockets, Bill looked at her with her up-turned nose and straight green gaze.

"Nerissa, you're overworking yourself," he said. She opened her mouth, but he kept talking.

"I don't want to have to use my key and find you've fallen from a ladder or something. Understand? So be careful," he muttered as he let himself out.

She'd done the work of three people and they both knew it. But he'd bite his tongue off before letting her know how impressed he was.

Chapter 6

She'd done it!

Bill Denton had been surprised by the appearance of the front of the house. So much so that he'd come over to tell her as soon as he arrived home last night.

His compliment on her efficiency was spontaneous. He even seemed pleased that the painting in the front room had begun.

However, when he saw all the other rooms she'd done, he clammed up. It was too much for him to acknowledge. She understood that. So he'd tried to make her feel guilty by accusing her of overworking.

It was ridiculous, of course. But it was his strategy to save face.

She moved the ladder aside and bent down to paint the final corner in the living room. Stepping back to survey the gleaming walls, she pictured them decorated with prints she intended to buy from local galleries. This room had to reflect her newly adopted Lowcountry home and future.

Buoyed by her good work, she moved her painting materials into her dining room and was soon engrossed in making the roller speed up and down.

She wondered if Bill Denton would continue to

ignore her rehabilitative tasks as she marked them off the list.

One thing about him. He might look like Ric, but he didn't try false charm on her the way Ric had. Bill was honest about his feelings and opinions. Brutally so most of the time.

He certainly couldn't be that way with his clients. Then why was he like that with her?

There'd been a clash of wills between them from the first moment. That had never happened to her before. The scary thing was that at the same time she'd had a physical reaction when he touched her.

The first time was when she tripped on the brick porch steps and he grabbed her to steady her. She'd not paid that too much attention. But last night, when he took hold of her wrist to prevent the brush from hitting his jacket, her response had been swift and positive, if unwilling.

Any other time she'd have instantly pulled away. But she had made the mistake of looking at his hand. It was long, smooth, brown, and well cared for. She could feel each of his fingers, the texture of his skin, so unlike hers, its warmth and firmness, its masculinity.

For a whisper of a moment, she felt caressed.

It was definitely time for a break. The fumes from the paint were making her fanciful.

She heated coffee and, seeing it was nearly noon, decided it was late enough in Seattle to call. Dad and her sister Alice were waiting for her to give them her new phone number. They'd pass it on to her youngest sister, Jan, whose insurance job kept her on the road.

The phone rang five times, then the invitation to leave a message came on. Nerissa obliged and hung up.

Tired of paint and inner analysis, she changed her clothes and went shopping. It was time to create a corner of color and beauty in the house. She had to erase the sense of bland depersonalization of too many motel rooms.

"Nerissa! It's time you called. We were getting worried about you."

Yearning for family filled her at the sound of Alice's voice on the phone. She'd spent last Christmas in Seattle, but that seemed a long time ago. Now that her quest for a new home was over, she had a sudden ache to see her dad, Alice, and Jan.

She stopped unpacking a box of books in her den and sank into a chair. "I had to wait until I had an address and phone number to give you." She passed on this information and told Alice how she'd found the house.

"So what is this Bill Denton like?" her sister wanted to know.

"If you saw him, you'd think he was Ric's younger brother. That's how strong the resemblance is."

"How awful! Why'd you rent from him?"

"I love the house and it's a rent I can afford."

"Have you asked him if he's related to Ric?" Alice asked.

"Of course not. He knows I'm divorced, that's all."

She knew she'd made a mistake mentioning the coincidental resemblance because her sister was a worrier, and loyal to and protective of her family. If she didn't put an end to this, Alice would work herself into imagining all kinds of dire scenarios.

"Listen, Alice, Ric married the girl and now they have two children. He's totally out of my life. You need to forget about him, too. Tell me about Dad and Jan."

"I might forget, but I'll never forgive him for not giving you the babies you wanted," Alice muttered.

"Alice. Please."

Like so many loving and well-meaning people, her sister unwittingly twisted the knife at the very core of the pain Nerissa couldn't quite dismiss. No matter how much she tried, with each advancing year she became more aware of her empty womb.

"Dad's okay," Alice said. "You know he could retire next year at sixty-five, but I don't think he'll do it."

After listening to the family news, Nerissa asked Alice about her two daughters.

"Grace is fine, into Girl Scouts and hockey, but that Lynn. When she turned fifteen, she seemed to think she was grown. Greg and I have to stay on her all the time, but she doesn't want to listen. It's just one thing after another."

"Things like what?" She sat up straight in the chair, a frown on her face.

"The latest thing is trying to make her do her homework. She wants to yack on the phone instead. Some of her new friends she's made this school year worry me. I've heard they skip school when they can pull it off. The way Lynn's acting, I can see her falling into that."

Nerissa twisted the ring she'd inherited from her mother. The modest stone was her talisman and a source of comfort when she was anxious. "Does she have any outside interests?"

"Not that I can see."

"It's early in the school year, Alice. Maybe she'll find something after a while," she said encouragingly.

She gave Alice messages to pass on to her dad and Jan and hung up the phone. Lynn, with her enthusiasm and initiative, had always been a special joy. It depressed her to think of her niece tuning out her parents. That could only lead to trouble.

Bill muttered a few pungent phrases under his breath. He'd purposely taken Dorchester Road home knowing the Friday evening traffic on the interstate would be bumper to bumper.

So here he sat, five miles from home, in a line of vehicles that weren't moving at all. He'd cut off his ignition ten minutes ago. Now he got out of his car as he saw a man walking back to the SUV ahead of him.

"Is it an accident?" he asked.

"Yeah." The man shook his head. "Looks real bad. They got ambulances, a fire truck, and police."

There was nothing to say to that except the hope that no one had been killed.

Back in his car he recalled his great-uncle Virgil's instruction when he took Bill, young and fidgety, to the fishing hole. "You can't move, so don't. Practice patience."

In this instance, patience was his only option even though he was about to be late for his appointment with little Breia, who was coming for a surprise photo for her parents' anniversary. Breia's cousin, Cherry, had set the time at six and now it was five forty-five.

He dialed Nerissa's number with the fervent hope that she'd be home. She picked up on the third ring.

"Hello."

"Nerissa, this is Bill. Could you do me a big favor, please?"

"If I can. What is it?"

Her voice sounded different to him over the wires, her tones more rounded, softened, not as edgy. A pleasure to hear.

He explained the situation and asked if she'd watch out for the cousin's car.

"When they get there, could you let them stay with you until I get home?"

"Of course. Have you any idea how long you'll be?"

"Hopefully no more than another twenty minutes or so."

"I'll take care of the girls."

"Thanks, Nerissa. I owe you one."

"You do, don't you?"

He grinned as he slipped the phone into his pocket. Nerissa was like a spice whose tang and fragrance, although not sweet, stayed with you after every encounter.

Fifteen minutes later, he called to say he'd finally started to move.

"The girls there?"

"They got here right at six."

"It'll take another twenty minutes. We're barely inching along. I don't know how much time the girls have."

"I asked. Breia said her mom told them to be home by eight. So don't worry, Bill. Get here when you can."

She'd called him Bill. Was it deliberate or had it slipped out because she thought of him as Bill? Nah. If she thought of him at all, it was probably as that mean so-and-so Denton.

But he pursed his lips and whistled to himself as he made his way home.

He expected Nerissa to open the door, but was surprised to see her with a girl on each side holding her hand.

As Nerissa introduced them, Breia said, "I'm glad you got here, Mr. Denton."

"So am I." He saw the girls were definitely of the type of African strain that he'd seen in the other Peebles family. Their sparkling dark eyes and cornrowed hair added to their appeal.

"Come on back, we're in the den." Nerissa led the way with little Josie, who'd looked at Bill shyly and moved closer to Nerissa.

"We wanted to dress up, but Mama'd want to know why," Breia told Bill. "Are jeans okay for the picture?"

"You look just right," he assured her, confident that her parents would be pleased with what his camera would see in her and Josie's innocent faces.

He took the three steps down into the den, thinking of how he'd compose the photo, then stopped in surprise. This wasn't the room he'd seen two nights ago.

This room spoke to him. It pulled him, and for a moment he stood still and took it in.

There was a welcoming couch, two deep armchairs, and graceful tables with shaded lamps. Vibrant color came from a few pictures on the walls, a nest of pillows in jewel tones, and the spines of books in two mahogany bookcases. An oriental rug unified the room.

His eye returned to the bold splash of color that came

from a long print showing a tall African woman dressed in blazing red, dancing. Her subtle sensuality dominated the room.

Emerging from his study, he glanced at Nerissa. She was waiting for his reaction. For a long moment they looked at each other, and for the first time, he saw her defenses down.

"It's a wonderful room, Nerissa." He let his glance touch her with warmth because his hands couldn't.

"I'm glad you like it, Bill," she said softly.

Everything about her at that instant was soft and feminine to him. Her green eyes lost their sharpness, her mouth curved sweetly, and even her posture became more pliant.

He had to tear himself away before he did or said something really stupid.

The little girls were talking to a young woman who had to be Cherry. She wore black leather pants with an emerald top that stopped just short of her navel. Her makeup was flawless on her smooth skin. Every hair of her trendy cut was in place as she glided toward him.

"I spoke to you on the phone. I'm Cherry." Her voice was sultry. Her eyes said she was interested in him.

With years of experience of young women practicing their wiles on him, he knew how to respond. Even though she was remarkably attractive, he returned her greeting with professional formality.

"We need to go over to my studio, ladies," he said. "Thanks again, Nerissa, for your hospitality."

At the last minute, Josie clung to Nerissa. "I don't want to go," she wailed.

Bill knew exactly how she felt.

He didn't want to leave either.

Chapter 7

This was one of those mornings when he hated to get up. Usually Bill was eager to see what the day would bring, what new places, faces, landscapes, and structures his camera would present to him.

But not this morning.

This morning he felt dull. Uninterested in the present prospect, unsure of what his next step should be. It didn't help that the sky was gray. Even the sun seemed unwilling to show itself. Fall was approaching, but here in the Low Country that shouldn't mean much yet. There should still be bright days with just a hint of cooler breezes and an occasional crispness in the air.

As he reluctantly rolled out of bed and went through his morning routine, he sought the reason for his doldrums.

Could he be coming down with something? A cold or a virus? He didn't think so. His usual robust health was the same as far as he could tell, and he was about to add to it by indulging himself in his favorite breakfast. Maybe it would make him feel better.

First, as always, strong, hot coffee. He sipped the brew as he prepared pecan waffles—his own, not a mix—smoked sausage, and a dish of ripe blueberries.

Business was good. He had a number of sittings on

this week's schedule plus a large wedding. Enough to keep him pleasantly and profitably occupied. He flipped the sausage over carefully, then turned down the fire so the meat wouldn't be ready before the waffles.

He added beaten egg whites to his batter and delicately folded in the pecan bits. The red light appeared on the waffle iron and he slowly spooned in the first bit of batter.

Occasionally, as he analyzed his finished photos, he wondered if he was losing his touch in capturing the essence of what he saw through his camera lens. Was that possibility underlying his somber mood? He'd been at this a long time and perhaps his eye was growing jaded.

That thought made him shudder as he filled a bowl with the plump berries he'd purchased fresh yesterday, sprinkled them with sugar, and, knowing he shouldn't, added a dollop of heavy cream.

He poured a second cup of coffee, put sausage on his plate, added the golden brown waffle, and, with a small sigh of anticipation, sat down to eat.

Maybe that was part of his problem. He'd been so busy with sittings, going to Columbia, and dealing with Nerissa that he had neglected his favorite hobby of cooking. Quick meals to keep hunger at bay had been eaten on the run without much thought.

His custom had been to prepare a meal for, or with, someone every few weeks. Sometimes it was a friend, sometimes family, or Chris and Maggie Rose. He loved to call into practice the careful blending of textures and tastes and colors accompanied by a flair of the unexpected.

As he savored the smoky sausage with the crisp

lightness of the pecan-studded waffle, followed by the special flavor of the blueberries, his mood began to lift a little. There was nothing like excellent food. It was a sensual delight that fed the imagination and the senses even as it nurtured the body.

True, it might add a pound or two that he didn't absolutely need, as in this case, but he'd never regretted the weight. Now there were some people who looked like they could stand a soul-satisfying meal. Maybe several. Like Nerissa.

She wasn't exactly skinny, but she was far from being what anyone would call voluptuous. Not that it mattered as far as he was concerned. But she was going to be too thin for her height if she didn't watch out. Maybe she didn't like to cook. Or she was so intent on keeping herself busy that she didn't bother to eat on a regular basis. He'd never known anyone as driven as she was to get things done. Just yesterday he'd glimpsed her surveying her backyard and making notes on a pad.

That space had never been planted with flowers since he'd been next door, but he wouldn't be surprised if that was what she had in mind. Everyone else had shrubs and trees, but leave it up to Miss High-and-Mighty to make it a showplace. He was sure going to keep an eye on that.

He was filling the waffle iron with its second stream of batter when the doorbell rang. He closed the lid and went to see who was calling at nine-thirty on a Sunday morning.

"Hi, Mr. Bill."

The teenaged boy with his red hair almost hidden under his backward NY Giants cap grinned a little sheepishly, as if uncertain of his welcome. His hands were in his jeans over which a too-large T-shirt dangled.

"Hi, Ross." It was the older Russell boy from down the street. "What can I do for you?"

"Can I talk to you a minute?" the boy asked, moving his feet a little.

"Sure. Come on in." Bill led the way to the kitchen. "Have a seat."

Ross sat down and sniffed the air. "Smells good in here."

"Want some? There's plenty."

Boys like Ross were always ready to eat. Bill remembered how he and his brothers had been at that age. One of his fondest memories while in high school was eating a meal at home and a little later eating again at Miss Pearline's or at a cousin's house.

"Thanks. I love waffles," Ross said with a big grin, and proved it by diving into his food as soon as Bill gave it to him.

"How's school?" Bill asked, making another round of waffles.

He'd met the Russells when he first moved to Tulip Lane and knew them to be a hard-working family doing their best for three boys and a girl, with education a high priority.

"School's okay. There's one class I really like, and that's what I want to ask you about." He took a large gulp of milk, burped, and excused himself. "In social studies we're doing a project on genealogy. This girl that sits next to me, we've got sort of a little contest going. She bet me that she'd get a better grade on hers than I would on mine."

Bill had noticed how Ross had shot up this summer. Yeah, the girls would glance at him, and he'd glance back. He had a healthy look and a wide, friendly smile.

"You're about fifteen now, Ross?"

"Just two months ago." He held out his plate as Bill served the last waffle. "See, I've got to win the bet, Mr. Bill, because if I do, I get to take this girl to the movies."

"First big date?"

"Yeah. That's if I win and if she keeps her promise, and especially if her parents let her go out with me. Alone." For a moment he looked glum.

"Lots of ifs," Bill said sympathetically.

Ross's face brightened. "I've been talking to Mom and Dad and my grandparents about our family history, and they've got a batch of pictures so that part's no problem. They even had some I'd never seen before of my great-grandparents who came here from Virginia."

"Can you use the pictures?" Bill pushed his empty plate aside. He was enjoying Ross's eagerness.

"Yeah. Mom had copies made and helped me figure out who went where on our family tree. I liked that part." Ross took his last sip of milk and set his glass down.

"Sounds like you've got it all done," Bill said.

"I thought I had, but last night I got this big idea of the one thing that will make mine the best." Ross put his elbows on the table and leaned toward Bill. "That's what I came to see you about."

"What do you want me to do?"

"Could you take a picture of our family? I want to put it on the cover of my report since it's the Russell family tree. What d'ya think of the idea, Mr. Bill?" He looked at Bill anxiously.

"Sounds brilliant to me," Bill reassured him.

"I can't pay you with money, but I'll do your lawn, front and back. As many times as you say." Ross beamed.

"When do you need this photograph?" Of course he would do it. It made him feel good to see that Ross wanted to do well with this assignment even if it was mostly to get a girl's attention. He'd already benefited by discovering information about his great-grandparents.

After they set a time and date for the sitting, Ross got up to leave. "You want me to do your lawn this week, Mr. Bill?"

"Saturday's fine."

"Thanks, Mr. Bill. The food was great."

"Just be sure you do a good job," Bill replied, pushing Ross's cap down on his head.

Ross's youthful energy lingered with Bill as he cleaned up the kitchen. But later in the studio, his earlier sense of dissatisfaction returned to gnaw at him.

Life had been fairly easy for him because he'd set his career path early and followed it steadily. Opportunities had presented themselves because of his talent and genial personality. Girls and guys had always liked him, and he got along with his many clients.

Finances were no problem because he'd been making money with his camera from the time he started college. Following his dad's advice and the example of his older brothers, he'd saved his money, then made small investments. They gradually grew larger, enabling him to become a partner in DB Enterprises. Now he owned two houses and had built a home studio.

So what did he have to complain about?

He wasn't sure. All he knew was that his filled

appointment book and his photographs on the wall failed to give him his usual sense of accomplishment.

Something had to change. He could no longer be content doing the same things over and over. They were okay and he'd do his best for Ross, but he had to find something more.

For the first time in his life he was aware of a hollowness. Maybe not that exactly, but there was definitely a deep-felt need for something to give his life more meaning.

Was this a midlife crisis? At thirty-four? This wasn't supposed to happen until much later. He scoffed at himself as he continued developing film.

Yet, in his gut he knew he'd hit a kernel of truth.

The installers had been delayed but had finally finished the new carpeting, and the hole in the laundry room had been repaired. What a big difference it made in how the house now looked, Nerissa thought as she began placing small items she'd brought from the storage unit. Tomorrow the large pieces would be delivered, and this phase of the work would be done. She stretched and raised her arms in contentment, allowing herself to smile. She felt like a cat who'd just had a saucer of cream.

Not an apt analogy now that she'd caught a glimpse of herself in a full-length mirror. She was almost skin and bones. No wonder her pants kept slipping. This morning she'd had to find a belt to put around her waist. Since the worst of the work was over, she'd have to get back to sleeping, cooking, and eating regularly. She looked old enough without letting herself become gaunt, too.

This was the first time she'd truly looked at herself in several months. She hadn't realized the physical toll the moving process had taken. Talk about something the cats drug in! Even her hair looked dull and ragged. But her house was almost ready for living. She pulled at her face in the mirror, deepening the hollows in her cheeks and under her eyes so that she looked really awful.

With a grin, she folded the last few towels and placed them in the linen closet. She bet Bill Denton never had a problem losing his pants because of lack of food. She'd noticed that his kitchen had a number of appliances, as well as some nice copperware hanging on a wall, so she supposed his girth came from the enjoyment of his own cooking.

Maybe, if they ever became friendly, she'd show him her cooking skills. He might be adequate in the kitchen, but she'd wager he'd never tasted anything like her marmalade cake.

That afternoon she made a pot of green tea and drank it leisurely while going through the recently delivered magazines to which she subscribed.

She looked with particular interest at the one featuring black artists and upcoming exhibitions, hoping to find something to see in Charleston. Nothing was featured, but an article requesting applications for a project concerning the documentation of places in Nova Scotia, Canada, where the Underground Railroad runaway slaves arrived attracted her attention.

Funding for the project came from a large grant available through the Arts Council, with matching funds from several other agencies and donors. It was to be completed in six months with the resulting exhibition highlighted at a civil rights festival in Detroit.

She'd never been to Nova Scotia, but she recalled several books that dealt with the history of how Harriet Tubman, after escaping slavery, went back to the South to lead more than three hundred slaves to freedom using a hidden system of safe houses and committed abolitionists. Some runaways were concealed on vessels going to New England. From there they were helped farther north with a small contingent ending up in Canada.

The article reminded her of a colleague who had friends in Nova Scotia and, returning from there one summer, had told Nerissa how she had visited a small town called Lincolnville, peopled by descendants of slaves.

What an intriguing subject that would be for some photographer. Suddenly the images of the pictures she'd seen in Denton's house flashed across her mind. Maybe he'd be interested in this. She looked to see if he was home, but the driveway was empty.

Just as well. She'd leave the magazine at his door with a note. That way she wouldn't have to see him or hear his usual putdowns.

Bill read the article late that night when he got home. He looked through the rest of the magazine, then scanned the story again. He went to bed thinking about it and in the morning read it again with growing excitement.

Here was something new, different. A challenge that was invigorating and unlike anything else he'd done. He'd been to Toronto and Ottawa during his college years.

Later he'd spent a weekend in Montreal with a friend and had been enchanted with its old section and its mighty cathedrals. All had been studies for his camera.

But he'd never been to the Atlantic Provinces. Maybe this was his chance. There was another reason he was excited. When he was Ross's age, he'd been extremely curious about Harriet Tubman. One of the social studies themes he'd chosen had been about her experience with the Underground Railroad. Her courage and determination had impressed him, and she'd stayed in his mind as a great woman.

How wonderful it would be to have a part in this project honoring her!

With the application form he'd have to send a resume, a one-page statement as to why he was interested in this and a portfolio of five examples of his work.

That would be no problem at all. The deadline was two weeks away, so he'd get right on it.

Thank God Nerissa had looked at the magazine instead of tossing it or putting it aside to read much later.

He really ought to do something to show her his gratitude. A simple thank-you wasn't enough for this opportunity that he was sure would be great for him. Already he could feel himself revved up in a way he hadn't been for ages.

It had to be something that would surprise and please her. After all, her bringing the magazine to his attention had certainly surprised and pleased him.

Suddenly inspiration hit him. He'd present her with a big bouquet of the kinds of flowers that she'd probably be planting in her yard.

Who knew? Maybe she'd even give him something he'd yet to see.

A real smile. Just for him.

Chapter 8

Nerissa's doorbell rang three times Tuesday. Each time she answered it, a significant event occurred, only one of which had been expected. The ring she'd been eagerly awaiting came at eight in the morning.

A broad-shouldered man in denims and a black T-shirt looked up from his clipboard.

"Ms. Ramsey? We've got your furniture for you."

Nerissa couldn't help smiling as she propped the door open. "Please come in."

The man and his assistant, a quiet young person, made it the least complicated move Nerissa had ever experienced. Each piece of furniture was set according to the detailed diagram she'd prepared.

She knew the only place for the deep blue sofa was against the living room wall so anyone sitting there had a view out the windows on the opposite side. This was a fundamental concept for her. Beds, also, had to be placed opposite windows, which made dressers and chairs easy to arrange.

In the dining room, the big table sat in the middle of the floor. Light from the French doors streamed over it. The maple hutch was placed on one wall and her grandmother's china closet on the other, exactly as she had envisioned it the first time she saw the room.

By ten o'clock, the men had been paid and gone. She began emptying the boxes, distributed in each room according to their list of contents.

Five of her favorite CDs—Mozart, Ellington, Carmen, Wes Montgomery, and BB King—provided inspiration and rhythm as she began the process of making the rooms of furniture into inviting, artistically interesting spaces.

At four-thirty in the afternoon she was pleasantly tired. The internal clock that had been driving her since six a.m. was running down and informing her she'd had nothing to eat but toast and coffee.

She was in the kitchen considering preparing herself a full meal instead of opening still another can of soup or having a bowl of cereal when the doorbell rang. A white car, unfamiliar to her, was in the driveway.

Breia and Josie were at the door with a woman who looked so much like them, Nerissa knew it had to be their mother.

"I'm Lucy Peebles," the lady said. "My girls wanted me to bring them over to show you the photograph they gave us."

She wore a black pantsuit with an emerald sweater that complemented her brown skin and eyes. Her shoulder-length hair was neatly cut, and as they shook hands, Nerissa noticed her nails were cut short and had a clear gloss. She had a familiar persona that Nerissa recognized.

She bent down to hug Breia and Josie, saying she was happy to see them again.

"You've got furniture now," Breia said, looking around the room curiously.

"It just came this morning," Nerissa said.

"Can Mama see the room where we had the hot chocolate and helped you with the books?" Josie pulled Nerissa's sleeve to get her attention.

"You must be very busy, and we don't want to interrupt you," Mrs. Peebles interjected.

"I'd stopped before you came, so you're not keeping me from anything." Nerissa let Breia and Josie lead the way while their mother thanked her for taking care of the girls the night they had to wait for Mr. Denton.

"Miss Nerissa's got a lot of books, hasn't she, Mama?" Breia said when they were in the den.

"Are you by any chance a teacher, Ms. Ramsey?"

"Please call me Nerissa. I've been wanting to ask you the same question. I'm a librarian."

"Ten years for me in the English department at the high school."

They smiled at each other, knowing they had shared experiences and Nerissa felt perhaps she'd found a friend.

"I was about to make myself something to drink, so how about hot chocolate for us?" she asked, looking at the girls, whose faces became all smiles.

At the kitchen table, Breia gave Nerissa the framed black-and-white photograph to look at.

Breia and Josie were not in the usual static, side-by-side pose. Instead they were staring at a figure on a pedestal a foot or so above their heads.

They'd been caught in a moment of breathless wonderment. Their small hands clutched the pedestal shelf as they stretched to see the figure more clearly. In their intent faces and clear eyes shone the heart-stopping innocence of childhood.

Nerissa widened her eyes to prevent the welled-up tears from falling. A swallow of the hot chocolate helped her get past the lump in her throat.

"How did Mr. Denton take this picture?" she asked the girls.

"We just walked around the room," Josie answered.

"He's got a lot of different things laying around," Breia added. "He told us to take our time and look at them."

"What is this you're looking at here?"

"It's a little girl angel," Josie said.

"She's holding a puppy that's been hurt and that's what she's looking at," Breia said.

"What do you think of your picture?" Nerissa was very curious to discover what impact the finished photo had on the young children.

"It makes me remember the little angel every time I look at it," Breia said gravely.

"Me, too," Josie said, "and how she loved that puppy."

A look of understanding passed between Nerissa and Lucy. "I've seen his work before," Lucy murmured, "but nothing like this."

"It's simplicity itself, yet has depth and poignancy." Nerissa handed it back to Breia, then invited them on a tour of the house.

Lucy expressed surprise that it looked so put together since the furniture had only just arrived.

"There's a bit to do still, and you can see I've boxes to empty and dishes to put away."

"Does that mean you're intending to stay in Jamison awhile?"

"Absolutely. In fact, I'm opening a bookstore as soon as I get settled and can find the right place."

Lucy's face lit up. "That's great. I have my list already of some black writers I can't find locally."

She gave Nerissa her address and phone number and urged her to visit. "Come anytime," she said.

She'd made a friend, Nerissa thought as she started once more to get something together for a meal. She felt a rapport with Lucy Peebles that boded well for a solid relationship, one she hadn't had since the divorce. It had cut her off from the circle of friends she and Ric had shared.

Then when Ric had moved in with his pregnant girlfriend immediately after she'd thrown him out, she'd felt humiliated as Ric and the girl had begun to socialize with the same people.

Not wanting to be the object of pity or ridicule, she'd absented herself and found, to her surprise, that there was no one she particularly missed or who, apparently, missed her.

It wasn't until later that she analyzed the reasons for that failure of friendship. Two friends in particular, Darlene and Carrie, had lunched with her often; they'd talked on the phone and occasionally caught a movie together.

Even they had faded away. Was she the one at fault? Had she been so wrapped up in her marriage that she'd neglected to put in the time and effort that developing true friendship required?

Perhaps so. But now she was reshaping her life, and with someone like Lucy, she was willing to work at being a friend, not just an acquaintance.

The dinner of steak, rice, and a green salad tasted delicious, and she savored every bite while reading a brochure she'd picked up at the garden shop next to the fixit store.

The dishes were washed and put away when the doorbell rang for the third time. She'd closed the blinds when it got dark so she turned on the porchlight and opened the door.

At first, all she could see was a bunch of flowers. Then they were lowered and Bill Denton's face emerged.

"Hi, Nerissa. May I come in?"

She stepped back, let him in, and closed the door.

"These are for you," he said, thrusting forward the large bouquet.

She instinctively took it but was speechless. Total surprise left her mute. Why was Bill here with this mass of beautiful blossoms? She sat down in the nearest chair, gazing at them in rapt admiration. Bill sat opposite her, a slight smile on his face, his eyes amused.

"I don't understand. Why are you giving these to me?"

"Because you deserve them," he said.

Now she was really confused. Did he mean because she'd put his house in good shape and this was his way of showing appreciation? That would certainly be a new tangent for him. She didn't believe it, but she'd ask.

"What did I do?"

"You surprised me and gave me great pleasure, Nerissa. I wanted to do the same for you."

She felt her face flush. Bill had never indicated that anything she did gave him pleasure. So far, it had been the opposite. And here he was, playing his usual cat-and-mouse game instead of telling her outright what he meant.

She wanted to be angry with him, but the beauty and the fragrance of the flowers were overwhelming her senses. She lowered her face and closed her eyes to drink in their exquisite perfume, to let it steal along her nerves and invade her inmost senses, to make her intoxicated with their sweetness, to drift in the scented air, released from her surroundings.

It had been years since anyone had given her flowers, and never had she been the recipient of such a large and variegated floral gift. White roses, red roses, yellow roses, lavender orchids, tulips, impatiens, mums, and baby's breath were mixed artfully with delicate greenery to compose a magnificent offering.

When she reluctantly opened her eyes, Bill was looking at her with a peculiar expression on his face, and his eyes were no longer amused.

She still had no idea about why he'd brought the flowers. It didn't matter. All she felt was the need to thank him. Another woman might prefer a piece of jewelry, but flowers had always touched her very soul.

"I don't know why you brought these to me, Bill," she murmured, her voice slow and sensuous, "but they're the loveliest flowers I've ever received. Thank you."

She smiled into his eyes and felt she could drown in the depths of his warm glance.

Bill was transfixed. He knew she liked flowers, but he'd never seen anyone respond to them the way she did.

First they'd robbed her of that fast, tart voice of hers. That alone had shocked him.

Then she sat down and buried her face in them. As he watched, it seemed to him she'd almost communicated with them in some way, but that sounded too weird. Then he saw her eyes close drowsily and a subtle change came over her as if she were intoxicated.

He wondered if she even remembered he was there, she was quiet so long, and she didn't ask him again why he brought them.

Clearly she had a deep passion for flowers. He doubted that she realized that it was so strong it left its mark on her. When she opened her eyes, it was transmitted to him in subtle but unmistakable ways.

Then she gave him a slow, intensely sweet smile. It was much weightier than the one he'd thought about.

He'd only hoped to tease her into giving him a friendly smile.

He was appalled to find that what he wanted, urgently, was to touch her.

Chapter 9

"I'm glad you like them." Bill was brisk, all business. No more of this emotional stuff. "I just needed to thank you for the magazine article. I'm going to enter that Nova Scotia contest."

"That's good. Have you ever been there?"

"No. How about you?"

"Never, but a friend of mine told me about a small place named Lincolnville that she visited. Escaped slaves established it, and some of their descendants still live there."

"Did she say where it is?"

"Near Halifax, the capital."

"I'll look it up on the Internet and see what I can find." He stood, looked around the room. "When did your furniture come?"

"This morning."

"It's very nice. Thanks again, Nerissa." He started toward the door.

She rose also. "Would you like to see the rest of the house?"

Are you crazy? he thought. That's all he'd need, to go into the bedrooms with her. "I have to go," he said. "I'll see the house another time."

He couldn't get away fast enough. He took in gulps of the cool night air and wished he had longer to walk in it than just across the grass. He sure needed something to clear his mind.

What in the world had happened back there? The question bothered him all through the evening.

True, he'd been without female companionship for quite a while. Even before Nancy had called it quits, he hadn't seen her for weeks, and not only because of his workload. There hadn't been any fervor in their relationship to hold his interest, but he hadn't realized it at the time. So he'd coasted along, now that he thought about it, riding the surface of easy companionship. Nothing demanded, nothing given, just mutually agreed upon enjoyment and entertainment. No lasting commitment and therefore no recriminations or broken hearts. Just friendly relations all around.

That was the way he'd wanted it and that was the way it'd been. For years.

So what in God's name was this reaction to Nerissa?

In the standard credit check DB Enterprises did on all their renters, he'd discovered she'd just turned thirty-nine. That was five years older than he was, not to mention that she had no figure, didn't know how to make herself attractive, and had the sharpest tongue of any woman he knew.

What in the world was he thinking?

How could he have been so tempted to hold her and kiss her and feel that skinny body melt against him?

It was beyond his understanding.

He should never have given her the flowers. Yet how

could he have known what they would do to her, and what her response would do to him?

One thing for sure he'd never make that mistake again!

It had been an aberration. That was it. He'd been tired, and she'd made her living room so welcoming and warm, and he had been really grateful to have this new project. He'd simply overreacted to her astonishing change from the unattractive woman he'd always fought with to a sultry female luring him with an enchanting smile.

It wouldn't happen again. You could take that to the bank and deposit it. From now on, anything to do with her was going to be strictly business, and even that was going to be kept to a minimum.

With that premise firmly in mind, he turned on the computer, got on the Internet, and searched for Nova Scotia.

Nerissa locked the door behind Bill and turned off the porch light. Cradling her precious flowers, she went into the kitchen and laid them on the counter.

She knew she didn't have a vase large enough to do them justice. Should she break them up into several portions and put them around the house? That idea had its advantages, but she couldn't bear to separate them.

Tomorrow she would purchase a suitable ceramic bowl. Meanwhile, she sought out her small bucket, filled it with the right amount of water, added sugar, placed the flowers carefully so all were erect, and set them in the unheated den.

Her movements were automatic, her mind shut off from introspection. She went to bed and slept dreamlessly.

The next day she found a silver and blue bowl big enough for two ceramic frogs with holes to hold the flowers in the container. She spent nearly an hour snipping her flowers and placing them upright in the frogs until they approximated the artful arrangement she'd received yesterday. She added water and the fresh flower food she'd bought, then set the bowl on a pedestal table in the living room.

It was just as she thought. The bowl enhanced the beauty of the flowers. She stared at them for several moments, beguiled in spite of herself.

Turning away abruptly, she went into her bedroom to resume putting away clothes, shoes, and bathroom items.

No music this time. She had to deal with yesterday, when her whole concept of what and who Bill Denton was had been turned upside down and inside out.

He had to be put back in his place so she could continue seeing him as the man who was almost Ric's double physically and therefore a nemesis. Each time she saw him, it reminded her of distrustfulness, betrayal, and shallow charm.

She needed to protect herself from him. If she let down her guard, only disappointment and hurt would follow. This she knew too well.

Ric, too, had made grand gestures meant to impress her and pull her closer to him. She realized later that they stroked his own ego, bolstered his self-image as a man who knew what women liked.

His gestures had tended to be lavish evenings at fine restaurants, or taking her to a big noisy party that someone of importance was supposed to attend. He would give her ornate boxes of candy even though she didn't care for them and had told him so.

But none of Ric's gestures had left her as weak-kneed and shivery inside as Bill and his flowers.

What had possessed him? She knew how special they were and how much they cost him. She was sure he hadn't told the florist to make him a "nice arrangement." He had to have selected them himself.

She couldn't fathom his true motive. Or message.

Not to mention what was in his glance when she opened her eyes to smile her gratitude.

What she saw then was the passionate depth of the Bill Denton whose insight and sensibility had made it possible to create the photograph of Breia and Josie's expressions of wonder.

That man was dangerous!

He saw too much when he bothered to look below the surface and into a person.

She deliberately stepped in front of her full-length mirror. *This is you*, she lectured herself. *Five years older than he is*.

Don't forget that.

As for the flowers, anyone can do something nice occasionally. Even him.

Her shoulders dropped a little as she assessed her image. Then she lifted her chin and went back to work, vowing that landlord and tenant could get along fine by greeting each other in passing and keeping matters on a formal basis if they had to discuss anything.

By the end of the week, all her cabinets and dressers had been filled. Art she'd brought with her hung on the walls. She walked from room to room, and what she saw pleased her.

At last she had a home again. One that was her own, reflecting no one else's influence. The apartment she'd lived in after the sale of the house had been temporary until she could move away from Minneapolis.

Deep in her heart she held her breath and noted the date. On this last Friday in October, she would begin to truly live again.

The next morning, she spent several hours in the large nursery she'd found in the mall. A knowledgeable clerk made helpful suggestions after learning what Nerissa had in mind.

Nerissa was itching to get her hands in the soil. When she got home, she had all the gardening tools she and the clerk had concluded she needed. While she didn't mean to be extravagant, she was determined not to borrow a single thing again from her landlord.

A green-eyed cat with dingy white fur sat on the fence watching her plant the azaleas.

"Hi, cat," she said.

She'd had a kitten once when she was eight, but it had disappeared and she remembered crying about it. This cat looked like it'd never had an owner. There was no tag around its neck and it was thin.

It jumped from the fence and inspected the holes she was digging. All afternoon it kept her company and followed her to the back door where it sat, green eyes fixed on her. She couldn't leave it outside. The least she could do was fix it a meal. And maybe a bath.

She went to bed dreaming of looking out her kitchen window and seeing white and red azaleas in full bloom.

However, in her first waking moment, the image in her mind was of Bill handing her a gorgeous bouquet.

It was Sunday, and as she ate breakfast, she supposed it might be time to get back in the habit of attending Sunday service somewhere.

In the past, she'd had to find a way to reconcile the teachings she'd heard all her life from the pulpit with the actual way people treated her. Where was the compassion that was supposed to keep people from backbiting? The kindness? The outstretched hands? Instead, the blind eye had been turned to Ric and the girl because of the innocent child about to be born. But what about her, the betrayed wife, whose only fault had been to love her husband and yearn for his children?

The peace she'd finally come to had been hard won, point by point, segment by segment. Those battles hadn't been fought in Sunday service.

She had wept, raged, and pleaded for inner understanding during many long and solitary walks. She'd wandered in parks, stood by lakes, stopped to look at gardens. Slowly, little by little, moments of peace came. They grew longer and more substantial.

Eventually she came to acceptance. She didn't fully comprehend why it had happened. She knew, of course, that it took two people to make a marriage and two to destroy it. She gave up assigning blame and trying to sort out who did or failed to do his or her part.

It had happened. It was over. Life had to move on.

Church hadn't played a part in her healing, and she didn't think it necessary now. However, in restarting her life in this new place she had chosen, it might be a good idea to visit around as a way to become acquainted with the community.

But not today. Today she had to continue digging in the soil, making a home for living plants. Knowing they'd be nurtured by sun and rain. Enjoying this October sun on her back and being thankful. This was worship enough.

Alice called that night, apparently at wits' end about Lynn.

"What has she done now?" Nerissa asked.

"She talked back to the principal and was sent home for two days. She said he was harrassing her about something he thought she was involved in. She declares she wasn't and kept telling him so. He sent her home for disobedience to an administrator."

"Is she still home?"

"No. That was last week. Now the teachers complain that although she comes to class every day, she won't talk. She rarely turns in homework. She just sits."

Nerissa said, "Trust Lynn to try the silent treatment."

"If she keeps it up, what will happen to her?"

"In your school system, I don't know. In Minneapolis she'd eventually be suspended."

"Suspended?" Alice sounded distraught. "Oh, Nerissa, what can we do to stop that from happening?"

To Nerissa there was only one answer. "My house is ready now. She can come here if she wants to. Perhaps a new environment is what she needs."

"Send her so far away? I don't know if I can do that," Alice wailed.

"Talk it over with Greg and let me know. The house is here if that's what you decide," Nerissa said.

Life was full of ironies, Nerissa thought, as she

pondered her future after talking to her sister. She'd get to enjoy her new house for only a few days before having to share it with Lynn, if that became the plan.

It was all right. Why else had she taken a house with three bedrooms? Subconsciously she'd known that some family member would be with her sooner or later. Her sisters were accustomed to turning to her when they couldn't solve problems on their own. She didn't encourage dependence, but she was always there as a last resort.

Lynn worried her. If she continued on her course toward a suspension, it could become more difficult to get her back on track. Nerissa had seen it happen too often. It was unfortunate she'd come up against the principal. That he would back down from his position was unlikely, and Lynn would end up with a reputation for rebelliousness, unearned or not.

If she came to Jamison before matters worsened, she could transfer into school here and continue her freshman year with a clean slate, free of the pressure she was under in Seattle.

The following Wednesday night, Nerissa picked Jan and Lynn up at the airport. They were the same height, which made them an inch or so shorter than Nerissa, but there the resemblance ended.

Thirty-year-old Jan, chic in heeled boots, suede coat, burnished curls and smooth makeup on her oval face, walked like a model and seemed not to notice the admiring glances as she came toward Nerissa.

Lynn wore jeans, black high tops, and a bulky jacket. The youthful contours of her face were set in discontent. Her lips and nails were painted black.

"I'm so glad you're here." Nerissa hugged her tightly.

"Me, too, I think," Lynn said, and Nerissa saw some of the uncertainty in her eyes go away.

"Welcome to the South," she told Jan.

"I've never been in this part of the country, so you have to tell me about it."

"I will, and I'll show you as much as I can before you leave."

She hadn't seen Bill in the past nine days, but as luck would have it, he pulled into his driveway as Jan and Lynn were struggling to lift a large bag out of the pickup.

"May I help you?" He hurried across the yard.

As Nerissa made introductions, Lynn blurted, "You look just like Uncle Ric." She blushed a bright red and, picking up a small bag, headed for the porch.

Bill raised an inquiring eyebrow at Nerissa, but it was Jan who explained brightly, "Nerissa's ex. Do you have relatives in Minneapolis, Bill?"

"None that I've heard about. Will you be here long?"

"Only until Sunday. It's Lynn who's staying."

He took the last of the bags out and carried them to the door.

"Thanks a lot," Jan said as Nerissa unlocked the door.

"I'll set them inside." He hauled in the luggage and glanced swiftly around the room.

His gaze returned to Nerissa, and she knew he'd been looking at the flowers in their blue and silver bowl. The awareness was in his eyes when he said, "Good night, Nerissa."

Chapter 10

"Which is my room, Aunt Rissa?"

Lynn had thrown her jacket on a chair and prowled around the living room, kitchen, and dining room trailed by Nerissa and Jan, who commented on pieces she remembered from Minneapolis.

"This one's yours." It was the next largest to the master and had a roomy closet and a window that looked out on the front.

Lynn immediately opened the deepest of her bags and pulled out three stuffed teddy bears of various sizes, a stuffed E.T., and a brown doll wearing a long white dress. She piled them on her bed, rearranging them until she seemed satisfied.

Nerissa reached into the darkest corner of the closet's top shelf. "Do you remember this one?" She gave the white teddy bear with "Hug Me" on it in red letters to Lynn, who clutched it to her chest.

"I thought I'd lost my huggy bear forever," Lynn said.

"I found it in one of my boxes that hadn't been opened in years."

"Now he can join the rest of the family." Lynn placed the bear next to the doll. "There. Now you can all get used to your new home."

***

She's going to be all right, Nerissa thought, after watching her niece's unconscious demonstration of coping skills.

"Dinner in half an hour," she said, then led Jan to her room. After getting Jan settled, she put biscuits in the oven, heated the beef stew, and mixed the salad. She'd baked an apple pie earlier and made sure there was vanilla ice cream in the freezer.

At the dinner table, Jan exclaimed over the food. "My favorite meal!"

"I hoped it still was," Nerissa said with a smile.

When dinner was over, Jan said, "Lynn, remember what you told me on the plane?"

Lynn looked at Nerissa. "I said I wanted to tell you right away about what happened between me and Mr. Bailey, the principal . . ."

Nerissa laid down her fork and gave Lynn her full attention.

"Teresa and I were on our way to English when we passed Mr. Bailey in the hall. Three boys caught up and surrounded us. I knew they were in trouble, and when they started badmouthing, I tried to get Teresa away. But she got mad and answered them back. A teacher heard the noise, and we all ended up in the principal's office." She shrugged. "That's all there was to it, but Mr. Bailey made it a big deal and we all got sent home for two days."

"Didn't Teresa tell him you weren't saying anything to the boys?"

"Yes, but he wouldn't listen, just like he wouldn't

listen to me when I told him I was trying to get Teresa away. This is the third time I've been reported for something I didn't do. I can't do anything right in that school as far as he's concerned."

"Did the teacher who saw you say anything in your favor?"

Lynn shook her head. "It's so unfair, Aunt Rissa," she burst out. "All I was doing was walking from one class to another! None of it was my fault. I went back to school because Mom and Dad made me, but I was too angry to do anything in class except sit there."

Her face suddenly crumpled up like a small child's, and she started to cry. She jumped up from the table, and a second later Nerissa heard the bedroom door close.

"Has she cried much since this happened?" she asked Jan.

"This might be the first time. Alice has been so worried because when she's home all she does is look at her TV or play games on the computer or read. And she sleeps a lot."

"In that case, this crying is what she needs, and I'm glad it's happened."

"I'm glad you invited her here. She needed to be away from the school before she exploded and did something that would land her in real trouble."

"Did you bring her transcript with you, Jan?"

"It's in my luggage."

"Good. I'll take her to school tomorrow and enroll her."

Jan began loading dishes into the dishwasher. "Let's talk about you now. How's your love life? Met anyone that tickles your fancy yet?"

Her impish glance was so familiar to Nerissa; it heralded a "getting into your personal business" from her younger sister. It used to be very easy to discourage her from this entertainment, but now that they were both grown women, Jan persisted until she found out what she wanted to know.

"What love life? All I've been doing is finding this house, cleaning it up, and moving into it."

"What about your next-door neighbor? I noticed there was no wedding band on his finger."

Trust Jan to check out a man's left hand immediately. Nerissa replied, "That's what he is, the neighbor who happens to live next door." She put away the leftover stew and the three biscuits Lynn hadn't gotten around to eating.

"How'd you feel when you saw his resemblance to Ric?" Jan leaned against the clean counter, her head tilted.

"To tell you the truth, it threw me. I started to turn and walk away. But I wanted this house."

"Did you ever tell him?"

"Of course not."

"He knows now. Poor Lynn. She was so embarrassed, but I can't blame her. I wanted to say it myself. Are you mad because I told him Ric was your ex?"

"No. Why?" Nerissa turned off the kitchen light and led the way into the living room.

"You never said another word until he told you good night."

"There wasn't anything to say. Now you tell me about your current love life. You always have something going on. Warren was the last one I heard about."

Jan had always been a social butterfly, never without a man or two in tow. So far none of her affairs had been serious. Nerissa thought Warren had sounded like he had staying power.

Jan's lively face became unhappy, and her fingers wound around each other in her lap. "We had a fight and he stopped calling."

"So you left town and came on this trip."

"I wanted to see you, too," she protested. "But the timing did come in handy."

"Was it so serious that you can't make up? The impression I had was that Warren might turn out to be the one you wouldn't walk away from."

"He *is* the one. I hope I didn't find out too late." Her voice was quiet.

Nerissa was searching for the right words to comfort her when Jan, who'd been gazing around the room, observed wistfully, "Warren used to bring me lovely flowers. Who brought you these beautiful roses? I thought you said there was no man in your life?" She turned a speculative gaze on Nerissa.

Nerissa felt herself blushing even though she tried to repress it. "Bill gave them to me."

"You mean the man you told me is, how did you put it, 'the neighbor who happens to live next door?' You can do better than that, Nerissa. This is me, Jan, so tell me the truth." She leaned forward, a teasing smile on her face.

Nerissa knew the only thing to do was tell her the whole story and hope that would put an end to her sister's teasing.

"I happened to give him one of my magazines about a photographic contest. That's his profession. He was very interested and is entering the contest. He brought the flowers to thank me. That's all there was to it."

"Really? Then you won't mind if I go out with him while I'm here?"

Nerissa was startled. "He asked you to go out?"

"Not yet, but you know me. He's an attractive man, lives next door. It wouldn't be hard to get a date."

"Feel free," Nerissa said. "I'm sure he'd be willing." In a flash she saw herself in the mirror beside Jan, with her curvy figure and come-hither smile. Of course Bill and any other man would choose to go out with Jan.

"I'm teasing you, Sis, but I am curious to know more about him," Jan said.

She'd like to know more about him, too. What did he think of when he was by himself? When his car wasn't in the driveway at night, was he out with Nancy or some other younger, vivacious woman like Jan? Did he ever feel lonely?

If he and Jan went out, Jan would learn more about him in the first half hour than Nerissa would in the whole evening. Men loved to tell Jan all about themselves. She wished she had that knack.

Yet it was strange how Bill Denton's personality had meshed with hers in a way that kept a spontaneous give-and-take between them that brought her a type of perverse enjoyment. She'd never let him know that. But from the gleam she sometimes saw in his eyes, she'd bet he enjoyed it too.

"How do you feel this morning, Lynn?" Nerissa asked as they climbed into the pickup.

"I feel pretty good, Aunt Rissa." She wore black jeans and a white T-shirt. Her thick brown hair was in cornrows, and the signs of discontent Nerissa had seen yesterday were gone. The bout of tears and the long sleep that followed seemed to have brought Lynn to equilibrium.

"I don't foresee you having trouble getting into school today, although I'm not sure what they'll do about the part you've missed. Whatever it is, we'll make it work."

"I can work hard if I have to, now that I'm away from Mr. Bailey."

"That's a good attitude, honey. Will you try to make friends, too?" That was what worried Nerissa.

"Sure. How will I get to school and back?"

"The school bus stops two blocks from us. That's how you'll come home today. We'll get that all figured out."

"It all went smooth as silk," Nerissa reported later to Alice on the phone. "They accepted her grades but gave a few assignments that she has to study and take a test on in order to catch up. If she can do that, she'll stay with her grade. She wants to do it, so I can't see it being a problem. We all know how smart she is when she's interested."

"How'd she act with the principal?"

"She didn't have to see her today. We spoke with the assistant principal and a counselor. Lynn was friendly and respectful."

"Bless you, Nerissa." Alice gave a great sigh. "I can't tell you what a relief this is to Greg and me. He told me to call him at work as soon as I heard from you."

Over lunch in a restaurant near Charleston's historic district, Jan asked about the bookstore. "Have you found a place yet? I've noticed a few empty buildings around here."

"My bookstore is going to be in Jamison."

"Why? Charleston is a bigger market, isn't it?"

"Of course, but it also has a number of the big chains. Jamison doesn't."

"I didn't realize that. Have you looked in Jamison?"

"That's my next project now that the house is settled. Would you like to go with me tomorrow to see what's available?" As an insurance adjuster, Jan would be able to give her some pointers.

"I'd love to. You know, Nerissa, I had no idea Charleston was such a small city to have so much history. The first shots of the Civil War were fired on Union troops at Fort Sumter in the harbor, and it has these beautiful colonial homes on Rainbow Row. What about the slave ships? Did they come up here to the water I'm looking at?"

"They docked at Sullivan's Island, which I'll show you before you go because I want Lynn to see it too. The slaves were quarantined there, then brought into what was then called Charles Towne."

The history lesson continued after lunch as Nerissa showed Jan the old churches and cemeteries, the Slave Mart, and the magnificent formal gardens almost hidden behind the gates of the antebellum and Victorian houses.

Shortly after they got home, Lynn bounced in, full of stories about her first day.

"I walked home from the bus with Ross Russell. He said he worked on your yard, Aunt Rissa. My English teacher was Mrs. Peebles, and she said to tell you hello.

She said she and her little girls were here not long ago.
I've got some chapters to read and tests to take, but I've
already looked at the work. It's not hard. The food in the
cafeteria is terrible, but at least you can buy pizza. Some
of the girls came up and talked to me. I've got one
teacher I don't much like, but that's no problem. I need
a new book bag, Aunt Rissa. The one I have isn't big
enough for some of these books. What did you two do
today? Is there something I can have for a snack?"

She seemed to have run down as she plopped herself
in a kitchen chair and looked at Nerissa as if she were
starving.

Nerissa laughed out loud, remembering how Lynn
could put on that expression all the time she was growing up. She opened the refrigerator door.

"Because you did so well your first day, and because
I haven't had time to shop for your particular tastes, you
may help yourself."

Jan remarked drily, "Just be sure to leave some food
for dinner."

"I don't eat that much, Aunt Jan," Lynn protested,
making herself a Dagwood-type sandwich. "I saw a cat
outside. Is it yours?"

"I'm not sure. I'm just feeding it because it's so thin."

"I like cats. They're so cuddly." Lynn bit into her
sandwich hungrily.

The next day Nerissa and Jan started their hunt for a
bookstore in the various malls that according to Pearline
Rogers had sprung up in the past few years as the population began to increase.

Every part of the town had them, and it took the
whole day to look them over. The largest mall had one

narrow shop, but when she called the realtor's number on her cell, the price was, to her, exorbitant. "I don't want to buy the place," she grumbled to Jan, "just rent it."

"They can afford to be expensive. Do you see the number of cars here? Look, there's a big movie theater with seven screens. Let's see what's playing," Jan said.

They drove by slowly and Nerissa was amused when Jan muttered, "I've seen that, and that, and that. Don't want to see that. Here's that romantic comedy I've been reading about. I want to see that."

"You're way up on me," she said. "I haven't been to a movie in months."

"You've got to change your way of living, Sis. Really. Don't let yourself get old and dull in your thinking. Let yourself have some fun in your life, because you haven't had any for a long time. I'm not going to nag you, but you think about what I'm saying. Will you?"

Nerissa was touched by Jan's concern. "I will, I promise."

When Lynn came home, Nerissa took her sister and niece to meet Pearline and Harold, who'd proved to be the kind of neighbors always ready to give any kind of assistance, large or small.

"They're such nice people," Jan said. "I'll be glad to tell Alice and Dad about your neighborhood."

"I want to walk around these two long blocks and see it all," Lynn said.

"You two go on, I need to start dinner," Nerissa said.

"I'll go with you, Lynn," Jan said. "I have to change into comfortable pants and shoes."

Nerissa mixed a meatloaf. She thought about Jan and

hoped she would make up with Warren, who was stable, calm, and crazy about Jan. He'd be a secure harbor for her in her more tempestuous moods.

She put the meat and potatoes in to bake and began to make coleslaw.

"You'll never guess what happened, Aunt Rissa," Lynn said as soon as she and Jan walked in the door. "We were talking to Mr. Denton." She flung her jacket off and went to the refrigerator for water. "He was getting out of his car when we came by, so he said hello and asked how we were and how did I like school. I can't get over how much he looks like Uncle Ric, but I think he's much nicer. Don't you?"

Nerissa began putting the food on the table while Lynn's conversation flowed on and Jan sat at her place, watching Nerissa.

"So then he asked Aunt Jan how she liked Jamison, and she told him how you had been taking her around. He said there was a big new mall, and Aunt Jan said the two of you had been there and she'd seen the movie theater."

As Nerissa sat down, Jan took up the tale. "We talked about what was playing and I said we were talking about that comedy and did he want to see it, too. He said yes. So we planned to go tonight, all of us. You don't mind, do you, Sis? Please say it's okay."

Nerissa couldn't say anything. Her fork was suspended in mid-air as this bombshell about going to the movies with Bill exploded in her mind. This was what came of letting other people in your home. You never knew what might happen. Jan was pleading with her, Lynn was eager, and what the heck. She hadn't thought to plan any entertainment for Jan, so what was a simple movie?

"Okay," she said.

Jan smiled. "He'll pick us up at seven-thirty, in time for the eight o'clock showing."

"What are you going to wear, Aunt Jan?" Lynn asked.

"I think the same outfit I wore on the plane. That should be all right."

Since Nerissa hadn't thought that far ahead, she said, "I guess I'll look at my extensive collection of jeans and pick out the least worn pair."

"Oh, no, you don't," Jan said. "Remember what you promised me this afternoon."

Lynn looked at them curiously, then asked Jan to help her pick out something appropriate. "It's Friday, and there'll be some kids from school there. They always check you out."

In her bedroom, Nerissa considered her wardrobe. Jan, smart and sexy in her suede outfit and high-heeled boots, would certainly flirt with Bill.

Was there anything in her closet that would keep her from being completely in the shadows? She decided on some double-pleat glen plaid wool trousers and a soft aqua silk blouse with a matching single-breasted flannel blazer with goldtone buttons and a notched collar. The aqua did wonders for her eyes, which had been why she let the saleslady persuade her to buy the outfit several years ago. She fluffed up her hair, put on a light touch of powder and lipstick, a whisper of floral fragrance, and black pumps.

It was strange about clothes, she mused as she consulted the mirror. She looked smart and assured, and therefore she felt confident and feminine in a way she hadn't experienced in a long, long time. Perhaps Jan was right.

Nerissa picked up her small black bag, turned out the light, and went to the living room. Jan was tweaking the collar of Lynn's smart denim jacket and saying something to her.

Bill stood by the door, and for a moment it seemed to Nerissa they were the only two people in the room, so strong was the tension that leaped between them. His eyes widened, and he took an involuntary step forward.

"Bill," she said, "it's nice of you to drive us to the movie."

"My pleasure. Are we ready?"

At the car there was a moment's do-si-do as Jan tried to maneuver Nerissa into the front seat beside Bill, but Nerissa, anticipating this, outflanked her shorter sister and seated herself in the back beside Lynn.

Bill ushered Jan in and engaged her in light conversation about Seattle on the way to the movie. At the ticket counter there was another shuffle as Nerissa and Jan tried to give Bill money. He simply ignored them, puchased four tickets, put his hand firmly under Nerissa's elbow, and directed the seating for Lynn to go in first, then Jan, then Nerissa, and then himself.

"You're pretty high-handed, aren't you?" she remarked silkily.

"You really think so?" His eyes gleamed in the half-dark theater.

"Yes, and I don't care for it," she flared.

"When you're dealing with Miss High-and-Mighty, you can't always be gentle."

Miss High-and-Mighty? Incensed, she turned to face

him, forgetting how close they were. He was waiting for her to do just that, his glance aware and amused.

"You look wonderful, Nerissa." His voice caressed her name. "You're so different and yet so much the same."

Her heart beat fast as she kept her face rigidly forward. *I shouldn't have come*, she thought. *I don't want to feel this way*.

On the screen in a coming attraction, someone was blowing up someone, the kind of movie she hated. It was followed by the comedy they'd come to see, and despite herself, she began laughing.

She felt Bill's gaze on her, then his large hand gently enfolded hers.

"I love to see you laughing and enjoying yourself," he murmured.

How could she relax and enjoy herself when he was holding her hand so possessively? She tugged at it discreetly. She didn't want Jan to notice anything, and she was sure Bill had counted on that. She glanced at him. His face was calm.

"Trust me," he said, a small smile quirking his lips.

She gave up the struggle and, with an unconscious sigh, relaxed and felt the release of the previous tension between them.

When they left the theater, there was no undignified scuffle about seating. Nerissa was beside Bill, Jan and Lynn in the back.

There was a four-way discussion about the movie, then Nerissa asked Bill about his contest application after explaining it to Jan and Lynn.

"I've sent it in. Actually, the hardest part was trying

to put on one page why I want to do this. Writing isn't my strong point."

"How soon will you know?" Jan asked.

"Supposed to be within three weeks."

"You're doing more research while you're waiting, aren't you?" Nerissa asked.

"I sure am. I intend to be ready when I get the word." He laughed. "I don't mean to sound so sure that I'll win, but I want to do this more than I've wanted to do anything else recently."

At Nerissa's door, Jan and Lynn said their good nights and went in.

"Thank you for coming, Nerissa," Bill said, and added, "our first date."

"Was this a date?" Jan was right. This man was too attractive for his own good. Or hers.

"Sure it was." His eyes twinkled. "And you're supposed to kiss your date good night."

He was so close, she could feel his warm breath on her face. It was ridiculous that he made her feel like an untried girl about to get her first real kiss. She took a step back.

"It was a nice evening and I enjoyed the movie, but I don't think it exactly qualified as a date," she said softly.

The laughter left his eyes and his voice deepened.

"Then go inside, Nerissa, before I kiss you. Date or no date."

Inside her house, she leaned against the door.

That was a close call, and although she'd prevailed, she couldn't help wondering what might happen on a real date with Bill Denton.

Chapter 11

Had she miscalculated her finances? Nerissa sat at the kitchen table and went over her figures again.

The house was quiet with Jan back in Seattle as of yesterday and Lynn in school. She'd been needing to do this since finding how high rentals were, but now she had trouble making sense of the figures before her.

She kept seeing Bill's face at the movie as he told her she looked wonderful. The imprint of his hand holding hers so firmly that she couldn't tug it away still made her tingle.

All through the movie, the connection had been there with its unspoken yet strong current flowing between them. He'd squeezed her hand once when she was laughing and said something about her doing more of that.

Jan had pointed out the same thing. Was she truly letting go of the fun and excitement of life? She knew it had eluded her after the divorce, but that was three years ago. Maybe she did need to loosen up, try to have more of a social life.

The cat Lynn had named Beans crushed against her and she absentmindedly patted its back.

She gazed out the window at the backyards, hers and

Bill's. There was a stout chain-link fence separating them.

In her fanciful mind, Bill was trying to break down that fence. First with his flowers, then his whole behavior at the movie, and lastly the kiss.

He hadn't actually given her a physical kiss, but his intent and desire had been so unmistakable, it was more than the brushing of her lips by a lesser man.

Nothing good could come of this. There was the pull she'd felt for Ric, only this time it was stronger, deeper; therefore, the inevitability of pain was greater.

Bill's resemblance to Ric was unfortunate, but it was like the fence, always there and unbreakable.

She tried to focus on her business spread sheets again. Information from the Internet and from the chamber of commerce had convinced her that Jamison was the small town where her money would go the farthest in making her dream become a reality. But now it seemed that dream might be in jeopardy unless she was extremely lucky. She hadn't realized that population growth had caused rates to double.

The move, of course, had taken a fair amount of money, but nothing she hadn't budgeted for. She gazed unseeingly at the trees while deciding exactly what she could pay for rent, insurance, electricity, a retail license, upkeep, and all the hidden costs associated with going into business. She upped the total from the last time she'd done this exercise.

Was she being unrealistic?

Her eyes brought into focus her new azalea plants, straight and green against the back fence. With attention and care they would be taller, larger, strongly rooted in the earth, and producing beautiful blossoms in the spring.

She would not give up on her bookstore.

Somewhere in Jamison was the place she could afford. She might have to postpone it until she could build up her income. She didn't want to, but she would do it if necessary.

Now that she had a backup plan, Nerissa felt encouraged. Tablet in hand, she set out to scour other parts of Jamison where there was enough foot traffic to make a bookstore feasible.

In the center of town there was an empty spot, but it was too large; there was a second vacancy next door to a bar. She didn't see anyplace else on this run and was heading home when she recalled she had bills to mail. The post office was on the other side of town, but somewhere near here she'd seen a substation. She saw the sign the next corner over. It was called the Mailroom.

She went in and put her letters in the mail drop, then went to the counter to buy a book of stamps. A nice-looking black woman who seemed to be about Jan's age greeted her. When she went to get the stamps, Nerissa saw she was pregnant.

"Is there anything else I can do for you?" She handed Nerissa the stamps.

"That's all. Thanks." Nerissa gave her the money.

"I don't think I've seen you in here before."

Nerissa picked up her change. "I'm new in Jamison." She looked around at the card rack, candy machine, beverage machine, copy machine, and in the far end a counter that said Craft Corner. "This almost seems more like a small store than a post office."

"That's how it started. It was a local store that sold a bit of everything. Then the owner added stamps for her customers who had trouble getting around."

"It has a nice atmosphere," Nerissa said.

"We hope so. Welcome to Jamison and come again."

As she drove away, Nerissa hoped her bookstore would have the same environment.

Bill was on his way home from one of the strangest sittings he'd ever done. It stayed in his mind for hours.

Mrs. Martin, a woman of sixty-seven, had asked him last week to come to her house as she wanted a special family portrait taken.

Her daughter had opened the door and taken him to see her mother, who was in a hospital bed with some medical apparatus around her. She neither looked nor sounded ill, Bill thought, and he was shocked when informed that she was dying of cancer.

Her face was calm, her manner cheerful. "They found out last month that I'm full of it, you see, but it doesn't show on me yet because I'm a big woman. I refused any treatment, despite my children's wishes, so I'm under hospice care. There's a history of terminal cancer in my family, so I don't see any use in putting myself or my family through a long suffering that's going to end in death anyway."

"But Mama, you don't know it can't be cured," her daughter cried out.

"Now, honey, we've been through this already." She held her daughter's hand. "I know my time has come, and that's why I want this family picture, Mr. Denton.

My four children, their children, my brother and sister and their families—I want us all to be together while I'm still looking healthy. My oldest daughter is going to help me get this together, aren't you, love?"

"Of course I will, Mama."

"What I wanted is a picnic, but it's too cool to have it outside, so we're going to have it inside next Saturday afternoon . . ."

Although the sun was shining fitfully outside when Bill had arrived at the house this morning, inside the place was full of light, music, and laughter.

Mrs. Martin, wearing a long floral dress, her hair looking shiny and clean, sat in a wheelchair near the fireplace, in which a glowing fire was burning. Children of various ages vied for her attention. She was obviously enjoying herself, but Bill could see shadows under her eyes that hadn't been visible the first time he came.

According to her wishes, he roamed the house, capturing the women in the kitchen making the potato salad and carving the ham. Two men were outside on the patio grilling the hotdogs and hamburgers. Other people spread the table with the kind of red-and-white checked tablecloth that goes with picnics, while some young people were setting up a sideboard with paper cups and soft drinks.

"Food's ready, come and get it," one of the men said, and there was a rush to the big table.

Bill was interested to see that Mrs. Martin refused to be placed at the head of the table. She wanted to be in the middle on one side, surrounded by her family.

The unself-conscious laughter, jostling, and joking of

the children helped to keep the emotional balance, although Bill saw the occasional surreptitious use of a handkerchief. The highlight of the afternoon was when Mrs. Martin started a story of an earlier picnic when one daughter had forgotten the baked beans and left them in the oven. The accused daughter responded by saying that it was her sister who had neglected the beans. That began a series of other stories and soon the room was filled with genuine joy and laughter. Mrs. Martin's face filled the center of his camera, radiating peace and love.

As Bill was leaving, the hospice nurse, who was just arriving, said, "I'm so glad she could do this today. Because she's not taking treatment, she's losing a little every day, and soon she'll be having morphine. That's why she couldn't wait to do this on Thanksgiving."

Thanksgiving was only three weeks away. Please God, Bill thought, he'd be able to spend it with his family, whom he didn't see nearly often enough. At one time he never let a week go by without seeing his parents, but the busier he got, the less he saw them. That was wrong and he knew it. He had to do better.

He had a box full of mail when he got home, mostly catalogs and junk. He put them to one side and looked at the letter mail. When he saw the envelope with the Canadian stamp, he tore it open. "We are happy to inform you," it read, "that you are one of our five finalists. The winner will be announced on November 15."

I've got to tell Nerissa, he thought, as happiness and excitement filled him. Stuffing the letter in his pocket, he flew out of his door, across the yard and around her pickup to her porch. That was when he saw that her door stood ajar and the smell of smoke lingered in the air.

"Nerissa!" he yelled, stumbling through the door. The smell was stronger inside, and he rushed frantically into the kitchen. There was a burnt pot in the sink but no Nerissa. She must be in the back, he thought, and then he saw her as he went through the dining room.

"What happened?" She was sitting awkwardly against the ladder, which was standing near the smoke alarm.

He dropped to his knees beside her and saw that her face was filled with pain and perspiration.

"My shoulder," she whispered through gritted teeth.

Without touching her he looked closely and saw that her left shoulder had become dislocated. From personal experience, he knew how severe that pain could be.

"It's dislocated, Nerissa. I'll call 911."

"No," she said, tears running down her face. "No."

"You've got to have it set, honey," he said gently. It was hurting him to see her in such pain, but this wasn't the time for her to be noble.

"Can't you do it?" she said. "I'll tell you how."

"Nerissa, it's going to hurt you so bad! I went through four years of football and I know."

"Just do it. Please."

"We have to stand up." He stepped across her and put his arm around her right side to gently pull her up. She took shallow breaths through her mouth and they were both sweating by the time he stood behind her, gently probing the left shoulder to find where the bone was sticking out.

"Ready?" he said and at the same moment popped the bone back into its socket.

Nerissa screamed and fainted.

Bill had thought she might, for he knew how excruciating the pain was. He gently lowered her to the floor, wet a towel from the adjacent bathroom, and laid it on her forehead. It was just as well. Her body needed to get over the shock. He wasn't concerned, and in fact as he watched and waited for her to open her eyes, it didn't do him any harm to draw some deep breaths and recover his own equilibrium.

He held her wrist, noting that her pulse was strong. It didn't surprise him. Everything about this woman was strong. Most women he knew would have been screaming with pain all the way through. But not her. She trusted him to reset it and that gave him a strange feeling inside. Thank God he'd been able to do it.

She opened her eyes and looked straight at him.

"How do you feel?" he asked.

"Better than I did, Dr. Denton. Thank you so much, Bill. I don't know what I would have done had you not arrived." She moved as if to sit up.

"Not yet," Bill said. "Give your system a little more time to adjust. What were you doing on the ladder?"

"Fanning the smoke away from the alarm so it would stop ringing. I reached over too far and somehow, in trying to straighten myself, popped this shoulder out." There was a sheepish expression on her face as she looked up at Bill. "This is the second time that shoulder has popped out, but the other time was so long ago, I'd forgotten it. I'm not going to forget again."

"Where'd the smoke come from?"

"A pot of beans on the stove. I can't imagine how I forgot about them."

"I think practically everyone does that at some time or another," Bill said, then told her about taking the pictures at Mrs. Martin's for no reason except to prolong this easy conversation with Nerissa. The setting was almost an intimate one with her lying on the floor and him beside her, holding her wrist without her pulling away.

"What a sad story," she said, "but what a courageous woman she must be. Did knowing her story make it difficult for you to do what she wanted?"

He stretched out his fingers against hers and looked at how they matched. Her question was one that people seldom asked, and yet it had much to do with what his camera produced.

"In the most important way, it helped. Once I got there, I tried to get inside her head, feel her emotions, and then let the camera see what she wanted to see."

Nerissa's green eyes drew him with their soft glow. "Now I understand how you were able to take that wonderful photo of Breia and Josie.

"I really must get up. I feel fine now," she said.

Bill leapt up, took her hands in his, and pulled her to her feet. He held her lightly as he announced, "I heard from Nova Scotia today. That's what I came over to tell you."

Her eyes gleamed. "What did they say?"

"I'm one of five finalists and they make their choice on November fifteenth."

She broke out in a big smile. "Congratulations, Bill. I'm so happy for you!"

"Are you, Nerissa?"

"Of course I am."

"Show me," Bill said huskily and tightened his arms around her.

He waited for the understanding to come into her eyes, and he held his breath. She put her hands on his shoulders and kissed him lightly. "This is for coming to my rescue today," she said, her eyes looking into his. She kissed him a second time. "This is congratulations."

Her kisses, light, sweet, and somehow innocent, nevertheless lit a fire in Bill. This time he kissed her, decidedly and hotly until she stopped resisting and her mouth softened under his. And her eyes closed.

"That," he said, "was because you didn't sit in the front seat going to the movies."

She looked so soft and bemused, he bent his head again.

"Don't push your luck, Mr. Denton," she said, side-stepping him.

"Don't you push yours, Nerissa, or I might have to rescue you again."

Chapter 12

"There's my absent boy," Gladys Denton said as Bill came into the kitchen of his parents' house.

Bill knew he was in trouble since his mom only called him that when she was put out with him.

He kissed her anyway, then leaned against the counter watching her slice the roast beef still steaming from the oven. He snitched a fragment to taste.

"Wonderful. There enough for me?"

"Yvonne was bringing her kids over, but they can't come, so I guess you can have their portion. Not that you deserve it, dropping by only every now and then." Her dark eyes snapped at him, and Bill saw that she was genuinely hurt.

She laid down her knife and Bill took her by the shoulders.

"Mom, I'm sorry. I get caught up in the job, but I promise to do better. Okay?"

His mother was a small woman, but the direct look she gave him took him back to his childhood days. From experience he knew she was wondering if she could depend on his promise, and it firmed his resolve to see his parents every week.

"We'll see," she said, patting his cheek. "Now make the gravy and help me get this food on the table."

Brian, the brother born just before him, and his two younger sisters, Roya and Bette, were also at the table. Daniel Denton, Senior, sat at the head and pronounced the blessing. Thinking of Mrs. Martin's family table, Bill echoed the blessing in his heart.

The conversation swirled around the table as the roast beef, mashed potatoes, gravy, corn pudding, collard greens, apple salad, and yeast rolls were passed back and forth.

Bette, who worked in an insurance office, complained about the sameness of her job.

"Have you ever thought about becoming a claims adjuster?" Bill asked.

"Not really. Why?"

"I met this young woman from Seattle who's about your age, and she loves being a claims adjuster. Gets to travel a lot, and she said no two calls are ever alike."

"How'd you meet her?" Roya asked.

"She was visiting her sister, the woman I rented my house to."

"How's that working out? She a responsible tenant?" his dad asked.

"Very. You wouldn't believe what the place looks like now."

"That so? I'll have to come over and take a look at it."

"Anytime." Bill wasn't surprised. For his dad, seeing was believing.

"She's living there alone?" his mom asked.

"Not anymore. Her high school-aged niece came to live with her."

It was time to change the subject. "I may be going to Nova Scotia soon."

Brian, who'd worked for Delta Airlines since leaving college, asked, "Where in Nova Scotia?"

Bill told the story of the contest and how he was one of five finalists. Although he'd traveled to other cities, this would be his first time to go out of the country on a professional trip.

"I was going to go with my senior ladies group to Toronto one time, but I fell and broke my ankle," his mother said wistfully after congratulating him.

"Would you like to go?" his dad asked. "We have an anniversary coming up in a few months."

When she hesitated, he said, "Someplace else, honey?"

"This may sound silly, but I've always wanted to take a cruise to Alaska and see the icebergs." Bill thought she almost seemed young again as she gazed at his dad.

"Alaska it is," his dad said. "I'll start getting the information."

Life had its ups and downs so close to one another, Bill mused that evening. Yesterday he'd come from a family dinner that had made him sadly aware of the brevity of life. Tonight his family dinner gave him a new light on what family in its essence meant to him.

Mom and Dad were more than Daniel and Gladys Denton. They had given him the foundation for the good life he now had. Dan Jr., Brian, Yvonne, Roya, and Bette were more than just his brothers and sisters. They were part of the fabric of his life and dearer to him than he'd realized, having taken the relationship, more or less for granted.

He'd seen Yvonne downtown last week, but he hadn't

talked to Dan for a long time. He got him on the phone and grinned with pleasure at hearing his big brother's deep voice.

"Hey, man, how you doin'?"

"Baby bro. Where you been?"

"Come on by for dinner Wednesday and let's catch up. Any time around six-thirty."

"Make me some of your steamed cabbage and I'll be there."

Lynn burst through the front door on Monday. "Aunt Rissa, where are you?"

"In the kitchen." Nerissa had become accustomed to Lynn's high-explosive energy. Eventually she'd try to tone it down a little, but right now she was delighted to see Lynn's enthusiasm.

"Guess what? You know those makeup exams I had to take last week? I passed them all. What can I have for a snack?" Her jacket and book bag landed on the kitchen table as she opened the refrigerator.

"That's great, Lynn. So now you're officially a freshman?"

Lynn sat down at the table with an apple, a can of soft drink, and a bag of chips snagged from the cabinet. "Yeah, and you know what else? Mrs. Peebles said now I can take theater, and the gym teacher said I can run track."

Nerissa sat down also. "Both of them, Lynn? Aren't they both after school?"

Lynn's face clouded. "Theater is the last class of the day, but once we start doing a play, we'll have to stay after, and track is always after."

"Which do you want to do the most?"

"I like both, but I guess I have to choose, huh?"

"Does Mrs. Peebles have a play picked out?"

"She said she's always wanted to do *A Christmas Carol* for the school's Christmas play, and this year she's going to do it."

"I can just see you as Tiny Tim's mother," Nerissa answered.

"No, I want to be one of the ghosts so I can scare everyone." Lynn waved her hands and, in a spectral voice, wavered back and forth until she and Nerissa broke up in laughter.

"I think taking theater is going to be more fun," she decided.

By Wednesday evening Nerissa was disheartened. For eleven days she'd scoured Jamison, searching for anyplace that she could turn into her bookshop. The most suitable places were filled, and the few empty ones were too large, too expensive, or in the wrong neighborhood. She'd been so sure that prayer and persistence would pay off. It always had before.

She wasn't sure what to do next. Before leaving her librarian job, she'd talked with the suppliers she knew well about opening her own shop. They'd been willing to open a personal account for her, but their offer expired on the first of December, a few weeks away.

Maybe she'd see if there was anything in the Charleston paper. She'd relied mostly on the Jamison paper and on her personal viewing. There was one company she hadn't seen before called DB Enterprises with both residential and business properties for sale. What caught her attention was that it had a Jamison number as well as a Charleston one. She tore the ad out of the paper. If they had a property for sale that was suitable, maybe she could talk them into a rental arrangement.

There was nothing else in the paper remotely possible. She glanced again at the list of shops she'd seen in Jamison. A feeling of despair crept over her. She'd been so sure of having a shop by now, yet all her efforts had produced nothing.

Lynn had gone to her room to do homework, but Nerissa heard her door open and her usual call, "Aunt Rissa."

"Here in the bedroom."

"I brought the mail in and forgot to give it to you."

The bundle was unusually large, and as she leafed through it, Nerissa saw that half of it should have been in the Denton box. Must have had a substitute on today, she thought. Bill's mail lay there on the card table while she took the junk out of hers, read her bank statement, and balanced her checkbook.

She sat a few minutes longer, then picked up Denton's mail. If he's home, I'll give it to him, she thought. Battling with him will keep me from sitting here having a pity party.

She combed her hair, brushed on a light layer of rose lipstick, and changed from her old T-shirt to a newer one.

"Lynn, I'm going to give Mr. Denton his mail," she called.

A second car was in his driveway and she hesitated, wondering if he was having a sitting, but as she stepped on the porch to ring the bell, she heard the hearty laughter of Bill and another man.

The door was opened by a tall man who took one look at her and said, "You must be Bill's neighbor. I'm Dan Denton. Come in," all in one long breath. He put his hand under her elbow and propelled her into the kitchen, where Bill looked up from a skillet he was tending.

"Hi, Nerissa. Meet my brother, Dan, who's going to get you a chair and something to drink while I finish this."

He sounded just the tiniest bit annoyed when he saw Dan holding her arm, so she thanked Dan for the chair and smiled when he gave her the apple juice. She saw that he was taller and slimmer than Bill. He had high cheekbones, large dark eyes, and a trim mustache, that looked good on him.

"Bill, I brought over your mail. Must have been a sub who put it all in my box."

"Thanks. I wondered why mine was empty."

"I understand you're from Minneapolis, Nerissa. How do you find Jamison?"

"I like it very much. I'm never going to have to wear a fur coat and heavy boots in the winter here." She smiled. What was Bill cooking that he couldn't come sit down when he had a guest, even if it was a neighbor?

"We were talking about the Nova Scotia trip when you rang," Bill said. "I'm trying to talk Dan into going with me, if I win."

"Are you in the same business, Dan?"

"I teach physical science at the College of Charleston. And you?"

"I was a librarian for years, but now my intention is to open my own little bookstore. That is, if I can ever find a place." Out of the corner of her eye, she saw Bill pour the contents of his skillet into a baking pan and shove it in the oven. He got himself a glass of juice and sat down at the table.

"Have you already looked for a place?" he asked.

"For the past eleven days that's all I've done."

"Here or in Charleston?" Dan asked.

"I definitely want to be in Jamison."

"Well, then, you can help her, can't you, Bill?" Dan looked at Bill, who was leafing through his mail.

Nerissa was puzzled. Did Dan mean because Bill knew so many people through his business? Whatever he meant, Bill seemed in no hurry to answer him as he opened a letter and extracted a check. She didn't need his help anyway.

She stood up. "I have to get back to Lynn. I have one lead to follow tomorrow. Maybe something'll come of it." She addressed herself to Dan, who had stood also.

"What lead is that?" Dan asked.

"A property agency called DB Enterprises."

The next instant, Bill was at her side. "Thanks for the mail, Nerissa. I was looking for that check. How's Lynn getting along?" he asked as they walked to the door.

"She's doing fine. Tell Dan I'm glad to have met him."

Once he was through at the stove, why had he hustled her out so fast that she hadn't had time to speak to Dan again?

Maybe it was because she and Dan had been enjoying talking, she thought with a smug smile.

Bill came back into the kitchen to find Dan waiting for him with narrowed eyes and a grim mouth.

"Why are you playing games with her, Bill?"

"It's no game, believe me."

"Then why didn't you tell her you're a partner in DB?"

"Because she wouldn't call them if she knew."

"I don't understand."

"Since the minute we saw each other, we've been at odds. If I said up, she'd say down. Just to be contrary. It's the weirdest thing, but believe me when I tell you, if I'm going to help her, she can't know."

"So you will help her?"

"Of course, Dan. There's a guy we're going to have to evict, and his place will be vacant in another week. I'll call Vince about it tonight. She'll have her shop tomorrow."

"Suppose Vince promised it to someone already?"

"Too bad. It goes to Nerissa."

What he wasn't going to let his brother know was that Nerissa had told Dan what she hadn't told him. It hurt his pride, but in all fairness, when had they ever talked as friends except when she hurt her shoulder? Then they'd talked about his dreams, not hers.

Now he'd have to find a way to get her to confide in him. That might be his greatest challenge yet in dealing with Nerissa Ramsey.

Chapter 13

"I brought you some coffee cake for your breakfast. I just took it out of the oven." Pearline came in and set the covered pan on the counter.

"Smells wonderful. You going to have some with me?" Nerissa filled the coffee machine.

"Yeah, I thought I'd have a bite with you. Harold's gone to the golf course and besides, I wanted to know how you're doing with your bookstore." Pearline took her usual seat at the kitchen table. "You haven't stopped by lately, so I figured you were still trying to find something."

Nerissa brought plates and silverware, cups and saucers. "I haven't found a thing, Pearline. At least nothing I can use." She served the fragrant coffee cake and poured the coffee.

"Did you try in the new mall? It's so big, there must be vacant places there."

"It was the first place I looked. Too expensive." She took her first bite. "Umm, good. I love the walnuts on top."

"It's an old recipe, but I like it. Did you ask Bill if he could help?"

That was odd. Dan had said almost the same thing last night about Bill helping her.

"No. Why should I?"

"He and two other friends own a company—DB Enterprises. They rent and sell all kinds of property."

In her surprise, Nerissa choked on her coffee. She ran to the bathroom, spit it out, and wiped the tears that had spurted from her eyes.

"Sorry about that. It went down the wrong way," she told Pearline.

"I've had it happen to me, too," Pearline said sympathetically.

"What were you saying about Bill and DB Enterprises?" Maybe she heard it wrong.

"He's a partner in it and they deal with properties. He doesn't advertise it, but I know he'd want to help you if they got any office space. He knows you're okay since he's already rented you his house, and I heard him bragging to Harold about what a good job you've done." She beamed at Nerissa with friendly pride.

Nerissa glanced at the wall clock. It wasn't quite eight yet, and she thanked God that Pearline had come so early. Nerissa had planned to call DB at eight.

She'd drop dead before she'd call now. She was so angry, it was all she could do to control herself as Pearline chattered on about her granddaughter and asked how Lynn was doing in school. Nerissa kept up her side of the conversation—but that deceitful Bill Denton! Why couldn't he have been honest last night and told her about DB? What was there to hide?

"Are you all right? Maybe this was too rich for you," Pearline said.

Nerissa tried to smile. "I think maybe I ate it too fast because it's so good."

"Save the rest of it for Lynn," Pearline advised as she left.

What hurt the most was thinking how five days ago he'd cared for her so gently and tenderly after her fall. She'd discovered an aspect of Bill Denton he'd never shown her before, one that she felt comfortable with, didn't have to be on her guard about, one she could trust.

The Bill Denton who'd asked for a kiss. She had given him two friendly ones. Then he had kissed her, and it wasn't at all friendly. It had been masculine, possessive, and worst of all, thrilling.

Now this. All he'd had to do last night was be up front about DB. What was hard about that? It must be something about her that made it hard for him to be direct. Yet he could kiss her as if he meant it.

She seethed with fury and hurt. If he had the last rental in town, she wouldn't take it. She'd find a way to build her own instead. She'd borrow from Dad if she had to. There *had* to be some other way.

Adrenaline surged through her as she scoured the center of Jamison again. There was one house that had been turned into a florist shop. She hadn't noticed it before. Somewhere there had to be a house she could use, probably on one of the side streets. But there was nothing. They were all residences, although a few did house businesses.

What was she going to do? She went through the malls again to see if she had missed an opportunity the first time. There was a new space next to a restaurant in one. She remembered it had been papered up. Now the papers were down and she gazed intently into the window. It was more narrow than wide but she would make do with it if it was at all within her price range.

It wasn't. It was almost twice what she could pay. Of course it had the advantage of being situated in a new mall that would be drawing hundreds of people each day. Plus, it was beside a restaurant that had already made a name for itself.

That evening Lynn found her very quiet. "What's the matter, Aunt Rissa? You don't feel good?"

"I'm just tired, too much bookstore hunting."

She was in her office going over the accounts when the doorbell rang. Lynn got to it first and she heard Bill Denton's voice; then Lynn called her. Two minutes before she'd felt drained and dull; now the sting of anger made her jump up, anxious to engage the enemy.

Bill was standing where Lynn had left him. She saw the hint of worry in his eyes.

"Hi, Nerissa. I came to see if you found a place for your shop."

"Thanks to you, no."

She had barely stepped inside the living room. She had to stay as far away from him as possible. She kept her voice low so Lynn couldn't hear their conversation.

"I don't understand," he said, anxiety visible on his face.

"I had cut out the DB ad and had intended to call the first thing this morning because it had a Jamison number. Then Pearline came over early, and during our conversation suggested I ask you for help since you're a partner in DB. Why didn't you tell me that last night?"

She could see his surprise. He fumbled for a reply, but she swept on, her chin high, her voice like ice.

"You've always been a difficult man to get along with, but I've never found you dishonest before. What is it about me that kept you from being straightforward last night?" she hissed, her green eyes blazing.

She had to wrap her arms around herself so he wouldn't see her trembling.

"I thought that if you knew I had a hand in finding you a shop, you'd refuse it. That's all there was to it, Nerissa." He looked guilty.

At first he'd seemed distressed by her accusation. Now, however, he'd shifted his balance slightly, straightened his stance, and was ready to meet her toe to toe.

She'd see about that.

"No. That isn't all there was to it. You decided, for reasons known only to yourself, that I didn't need that information. That I'm not capable of making my own decisions. Even Dan, whom I'd just met, gave me more credit than that when he said that you could help me. He expected you to tell me. You're a deceitful man, Mr. Denton. I'm sure you can find your way out."

She turned quickly and went back to her office, not waiting to see what he did. After a long moment, she heard the front door close.

In an effort to stop her sudden shivering, she had a mug of scalding tea, then called home, seeking comfort from knowing that there was a place she belonged and where she was loved unconditionally.

Alice answered and said, "Wait a sec, let me tell Greg to pick up the other phone." Nerissa welcomed Greg's calmness, which was a perfect foil to Alice's intensity.

"Nerissa, I hope Lynn isn't upsetting your life too much," he said.

"Tell the truth now, Nerissa," Alice said, anxiety in her voice.

"Naturally I've had to make some adjustments, but we're getting along fine. I'm glad you sent her the phone card, and I expect she's told you how she passed her makeup exams and is a full freshman now."

"She told us last night and she also mentioned getting in the theater class. Remember when she was little and loved to put on plays she made up? I bet she'll be good in that class," Alice said.

Greg chuckled. "She said she wanted to be one of the ghosts."

"She said she's made friends on your street." This from Alice.

"Mentioned a boy named Ross. You know him?" Greg asked.

"Ross cuts my grass. I've been to the house, and they're a nice family."

"I miss her so much. We all do." Alice's voice got a little shaky. "Does she seem homesick?"

"I can tell she is when she gets quiet and sits around holding her stuffed animals."

"We're bringing her home for the Thanksgiving weekend," Greg said.

"She'll love that. Have you told her?"

"Not yet. One other thing, Nerissa. She has her phone card and allowance. If you ever need more than the monthly check I'm sending you, all you have to do is let me know." He chuckled again. "Of course, she'd like to have her own credit card, but I told her that was out of the question at her age.

"Thanks again, Nerissa. You're the only person we'd let our Lynn go to."

The sincerity and warmth in Greg's voice were just what Nerissa needed, and as she and Alice talked for another half hour about Grace, Jan's trip, Alice's job, and the hunt for the bookstore, those feelings carried over, surrounding her in the essence of familial affection.

After Alice hung up, Nerissa dialed her dad's number. He was hard to catch since he involved himself in service organizations that filled his non-working hours.

When she heard his "hello," she was suddenly so filled with emotion that she could hardly speak.

"It's me, Dad. Nerissa."

"Puddin'. How wonderful to hear your voice. How's everything going?"

His own name for her, spoken in his tender, velvety voice, reduced her to tears. She couldn't help but sniff as she dug in her pocket for a tissue.

"Why're you crying, baby? What's wrong?" Now he sounded alarmed.

Through her tears she managed to say, "I'm okay, Dad. This is just one of those days when you're too far away."

There was silence for a moment while she wiped her eyes and blew her nose.

"That's every day for me, Nerissa, but I understand why you made your choice. Is Lynn giving you trouble?"

"Not at all. I just got through talking with Alice and Greg. They can give you the news about Lynn."

"What else is happening that's upset you, Puddin'? I know it's more than loneliness."

She wasn't surprised at his perceptiveness. He'd always been able to read her. They were a lot alike, she and her dad.

"My house is finished now, so I've moved on to getting my bookshop set up. The problem is, I can't find a single place to rent. I've been to the malls and everywhere else in Jamison, several times over. There isn't a place that's suitable that I can afford. Nothing. I guess I'm a little down about it because you know how carefully I've been planning for this." She had consulted her dad about her business plan several times.

He asked her questions about the town's layout and the traffic patterns. After discussing the matter for some minutes, he said, "You want my suggestion?"

"Of course, Dad."

"You have two options. Wait until something becomes available or decide to buy a place. If you need to buy, Nerissa, you know I'm behind you. We'll work out details. I want you to have your bookshop, Puddin'."

She laid the phone down gently after the conversation was over and thought about her dear family.

Later, getting ready for bed, she felt cleansed inside as well as outside, thankfully emptied of the anger and hurt that had erupted in her.

Her bruised heart would take longer to heal.

Chapter 14

Bill closed Nerissa's door behind him, stunned by her dismissal. She hadn't even let him explain thoroughly why he hadn't told her he was a part of DB. Knowing how the two of them were usually at odds with each other because of her strong independent streak, surely she could see why he intended to help her in a less direct way.

Women! As he stomped up his steps and into his house, he could only think how difficult they were to understand. Of course he was going to see that she had a rental property for her bookstore. Why couldn't she just have accepted that?

No, she had to get all high-and-mighty again and accuse him of always being a difficult man to get along with when everybody knew he was friendly and easy. And then she had the nerve to call him deceitful and dishonest. That really hurt!

In his personal relationships and in his business, he'd made it a habit of being the opposite, of being honest and trustworthy, because those were his own values. It was how he'd been raised and what he as an individual truly believed in.

He dropped down on the sofa and stretched his legs out. He'd called Vince that morning to alert him about the call from Nerissa, but he hadn't been able to check with DB before the close of business. So he'd gone next door expecting to hear that she'd found a place and, of course, he'd decided to not mention his part in it.

So when she'd said that thanks to him she *hadn't* found a place, he'd been surprised. Then when she lashed out at him because, among other reasons, he thought she wasn't capable of making her own decisions, he would have laughed had he not been so distressed. He'd never met a woman who was more capable of making up her own mind.

Now, in her estimation, he was so far out in the cold that he might never get back in.

His shoulders slumped. They'd been making progress toward a more friendly relationship. Only a few days ago she'd trusted him to help her when she'd fallen from the ladder. They'd talked like friends, and she'd shown such understanding of his work.

To his own surprise he'd almost teasingly asked for a kiss when she said she was grateful. She'd given him two in a sweet way that had fired him up to give her a real one that had made him want more. He'd been stunned at his reaction.

Since then he'd been planning on when he could repeat that exercise, for underneath all her tartness and sharpness was this sweetness that had a freshness about it. She'd been married, he knew, but he'd sure like to know more than just that fact. What kind of marriage had it been? What sort of guy was her ex?

He sensed an innocence about her, but not only that. A woman like her would also be passionate with that sweetness. None of the women he'd known had the combination of qualities that Nerissa had, and he longed to explore them.

She was a challenge to his masculinity, but there was more to it than that, he decided. He got up from the sofa, too restless to sit. He wandered into the kitchen and stood by the sink, gazing at her house. She drew him. Unwillingly. He wasn't ready to be deeply serious about a woman, but with Nerissa he didn't seem to have much choice.

That combination of intelligence, feistiness, and inner sweetness fascinated him. Add to that her expressive green eyes, her long legs, and the way she never backed down, no matter what he threw at her, and it made an unbeatable combination.

He'd blown it all away. How could he have been so stupid?

He felt like hammering his head against the wall. He doubted that would help, so he did the next best thing and made a pot of very strong coffee. As he drank cup after cup, he admitted he'd been all kinds of a fool, that he had indeed failed to let Nerissa decide what to do about him and DB, and that now his urgent goal was to make this right. Somehow.

How could he heal the rift he'd caused between them?

"Aunt Rissa, in social studies we have to do a report on a business," Lynn said, snatching a french fry from the dish Nerissa was getting ready to put on the table. "Ross and I don't want to choose a local store like everyone else. Ross said he'd been to a riding stable once. We'd like to go there for our report. Can you take us? Please?"

"Does he know where it is?" She'd only seen one

stable as she rode around Jamison. Maybe that was the one Ross meant.

"He said he'd make sure of the directions. It's a little ways out of town."

The arrangements were made and now, on this bright Saturday morning, Nerissa was driving Lynn and Ross on a country road, glad to be doing something different and getting away from the anxiety of finding a rental and worrying about her disappointment with Bill.

At the sign "HS Stables," she turned right onto a long gravel road with a large field on the left side.

Lynn pointed to it excitedly. "Look! There's kids riding those horses. They look like they're our age."

"It's a riding school, and anyone can take lessons," Ross said.

On the right as they approached the house was a small building with the sign HS STABLES OFFICE. Almost before Nerissa could stop her pickup, Ross and Lynn were out and had gone over to lean on the fence and watch the riders.

Nerissa walked into the office, which was comfortably furnished with several straight chairs, a sofa, and a large desk flanked by file cabinets.

A young black woman greeted her from behind the desk as Nerissa said her name and explained that she'd brought two students who wanted to do a report on the business for their social studies class.

"Nerissa Ramsey? You must be the lady Bill Denton's been telling us about, the one who rented his house," the lady said with a pleased smile. "I'm so glad to meet you."

He's been talking about me to people, she thought,

and couldn't help her expression turning sober. The lady instantly reacted.

"Oh, I'm so sorry. I don't mean to imply that he was gossiping." She turned red and came from around the desk to apologize again. "Please forgive me. Bill and my husband Chris are best friends. I'm Maggie Rose Shealy."

Nerissa recognized her as the pregnant woman from the Mailroom. "I guess we're even because I heard about you and your husband from Pearline Rogers."

"Chris is going to be so disappointed at not meeting you, but this is his busiest day and he's all over the place, from one student to another. Let me take you outside and show you and your students around," Maggie Rose said.

At the end of the tour, Lynn and Ross were both asking the price of lessons and wondering how they could fit them into their crowded days.

Maggie Rose answered their specific questions about the size of the property that was used for the stables, the number of students, and the number of instructors.

They already had learned the horses' names and recited them for Maggie Rose to see if they were correct.

"The biggest one is HS. The silvery gray is Starlight. The real graceful one is Windsong. Then there's Chica, and Nicky is the pony for the little kids."

"Correct. You both get an A-plus," Maggie Rose said.

"How much more time do we have, Aunt Rissa?" Lynn asked.

"I'm going to talk with Mrs. Shealy a little, so stay in sight and I'll call you."

"It seems to me they're going to give a good report," Maggie Rose observed as she led Nerissa back into the office and sat beside her on the sofa. "This suits me nowadays."

"How are you getting along? You're pretty busy working here and in the Mailroom, where you're on your feet." Deprived of children of her own, Nerissa instinctively reacted protectively toward pregnant women.

"I'm just fine, but I've promised Chris that I'd consult our physician around the eighth month about continuing both jobs." She rubbed her belly a little. "The baby's active today."

"Is it a boy or a girl?"

"We agreed not to find out. As long as it's healthy, that's all that matters." She shifted to another position. "But what about you? Are you liking Jamison?"

"I like it very much. Now that I'm settled in the house, I'm getting ready to open a bookstore."

By the time they'd discussed this piece of news and Maggie Rose had congratulated Nerissa and offered any help she could provide, it was time to go home.

Lynn and Ross plotted their report all the way home while Nerissa thought about how Bill, Chris, and Maggie Rose had grown up together. When you've known each other all your life, you know if a person is deceitful or dishonest.

She could have asked Maggie Rose her opinion about Bill Denton, but a question like that was too personal. Not only that, he might never show that aspect of himself to her or Chris.

What she had to go by was that he'd shown it to her, and she'd never forgive him!

Chapter 15

First the shower was too cold, then too hot. Nerissa couldn't seem to get it right. All she wanted was to feel refreshed enough to start this new day. She'd gone to bed tired from her gardening and had fallen right to sleep. For two hours. The rest of the night had been full of turning, twisting, having disastrous thoughts about her bookstore, trying to be optimistic about the bookstore, and wondering why was it so difficult for her to have a male friend.

She felt terrible. Her mind was blank as the water poured over her until she turned it off. After drying herself, she examined her face in the mirror and then wished she hadn't. This morning she didn't look like nearly forty, she looked more like a definite forty-five with the lines around her mouth and nose and the beginning of circles under her eyes.

Maybe if she took the time to make herself look good, she'd feel good. She dressed herself in black pants, a cranberry knit shirt with matching earrings, and black slip-ons with a little heel. Then she spent time on her face and her hair. She stepped back and assessed her appearance in the full-length mirror.

It worked. She looked like an attractive woman who had a confident air. Pleased with herself, she left her bedroom thinking this had to become her routine once she opened her bookstore.

After their leisurely Saturday breakfast of sausage, scrambled eggs, home fries, and bagels, she dropped Lynn off at the home of her friend Keisha, then did her survey.

As she passed a jewelry store, she was reminded that Jan was having a birthday next week, so she parked and went in. She enjoyed looking, but the prices were too high. She could send something else, but Jan loved jewelry of all kinds. The Mailroom had a counter where local crafts were sold. She'd try there.

The place was doing a brisk business at the mail counter. The stately woman at the craft counter smiled and said, "Good morning. I'm Helen Reid. I don't believe I've seen you here before."

"I'm Nerissa Ramsey. I was at the mail counter once but not over here. This is such a novel idea, selling crafts in a post office."

"Yes, it is, but it's working out successfully. The original owner had the post office here for many years and sold it to her niece when she retired."

"Would that be Mrs. Shealy?"

"The niece is Ginnie Steed, the lady at the farthest cash register. Maggie Rose is her partner. This craft corner is their addition to the business. Are you looking for something in particular, Miss Ramsey?"

During the conversation, Nerissa had been fascinated by the variety and originality of vases, bowls, small animals, flowers, tableware, candlesticks, and jewelry on display.

"Jewelry for my sister."

"What kind does she like?" Mrs. Reid asked.

"She wears all sorts according to her mood and her outfit. Could I see that emerald-looking bracelet?"

Nerissa was enjoying herself talking to Mrs. Reid as they looked at jewelry. This was relaxing and so different from what she'd been doing for days.

"I'm taking up too much of your time," she apologized.

"Not at all. I like doing this, otherwise I'd be sitting in my chair hoping for someone like you to come along. You live in Jamison?"

"I do now. I'm going to open a bookstore."

Mrs. Reid smiled broadly. "Good. I love to read, and all my grandchildren receive books from me for their birthdays. Where is your store?"

"I'm having a problem finding a place to rent. I've been looking for weeks all over Jamison, but so far, no luck." She fingered the pendant on the counter. It was a square of silver with a scroll motif hanging from a black silk cord. Jan wore a lot of black, and this would be striking on her.

"What kind of rental space were you wanting, Miss Ramsey?"

Nerissa heard something in her voice that made her pay attention.

"At this point, I'll consider almost anything I can pay for. My only need is for it to be in the central part of Jamison. Do you know of a place, Mrs. Reid?" She felt like she wanted to hold her breath.

"I think I might. My 92-year-old aunt is moving to an assisted living place, and her house will be up for rent. Can you use a house?"

"Where is it?"

"One block off Main Street. It's one of the few residences left on the street."

"Is it very big?"

"Five rooms plus bath, all on one floor."

"It sounds almost too good to be true. No one in your family wants it?"

"We all have our own homes, but we don't want to sell Auntie's and we've been talking about finding a tenant we can depend on. Why don't you give me your name and number and I can call you after I talk to the family?"

As the exchange of phone numbers was made, Nerissa asked if she could drive by to look at the house from the outside.

"Of course," Mrs. Reid said and wrote the address on a card.

"I've been out to the Shealy place, so you can ask Maggie Rose about me and I can give you other references if this works out," Nerissa said.

When she picked Lynn up, she was still too keyed up to go home.

"We don't have to go home yet. What would you like to do?"

"Could we go to the new mall, Aunt Rissa?"

"Sure. Any particular store?" She grinned at Lynn's curious glance. Mall shopping was not usually high on Nerissa's list.

"That new teen store next to the big department store. All the kids at school are talking about it."

After they had decided whether or not they liked most of the items in the store, Lynn announced she was hungry.

"I am too," Nerissa said. "Let's go to a restaurant here instead of going home."

"Did something special happen today?" Lynn asked.

"Yes. I think I found my bookstore."

"Wow! Where? That's so exciting!"

It wasn't hard for Lynn to sense Nerissa's excitement. But as Lynn listened to Nerissa's story over dinner and asked questions about what would happen next and how could she help and what would this mean to their usual routine, Nerissa sensed that Lynn had a basic understanding about the hard work involving long hours and giving up some leisure activities that were involved.

They lingered over cherry pie à la mode. Nerissa felt she deserved this indulgence. If she got the house, it would be months before she'd be able to do this again.

It was dark by the time they got home.

"I hardly ever see Mr. Bill's car anymore," Lynn remarked, raking a wad of papers and mail from the box.

Among the catalogs and bills, Nerissa found a square white envelope with her name on it. She recognized the writing and her heart beat faster. Lynn was saying something about a pair of shoes advertised in the paper. Nerissa put the envelope aside.

In the privacy of her bedroom, she slit the envelope and drew out a folded note.

Nerissa, I wanted you to know that I won the contest.
I wouldn't have known about it had it not been for you.
Thank you again with all of my heart.
                                        Bill

He'd won! For a long moment, she held the note against her heart and smiled.

Chapter 16

Ross came to see Bill Saturday afternoon. They stood in the backyard looking at the leaves.

"I can rake those for you, Mr. Bill. I still owe you at least one more yard job for the picture."

"What happened with that? Did you take the girl out?" Bill asked.

"I got the best grade and we went to the movies," he said dismissively.

"Didn't work out, huh?" Bill gave him a man-to-man glance.

"She's kinda stuck up," Ross said with a shrug.

"Haven't I seen you with Lynn?" He'd noticed them a time or two walking down the street.

"Yeah. We're in the same grade and ride the bus together. She's fun and interesting. Maybe it's because she's from Seattle."

Bill found Ross's naiveté endearing. "Interesting like how?"

"We had to do a report on some kind of business, and she got Miss Nerissa to take us to the HS Stables."

That was a jolt. So Nerissa had met Maggie Rose and Chris. What, he wondered, had they thought of each other?

Ross went to the shed for the rake. Nerissa's driveway

was empty, but who knew? Maybe while Ross was still here, Lynn would return and they'd talk. It was an indirect way to discover if Nerissa had found her bookstore, but at least he'd know.

Sunday morning found Nerissa and Lynn in church with Lucy Peebles and her family. Lucy's husband, Benjamin, turned out to be as friendly as Lucy. Breia and Josie were excited to see her, and after the service they stood in a group talking about the Christmas play, while Lucy introduced other people as they stopped by.

"That was nice," Lynn chattered on the way home. "Breia and Josie are so cute."

Nerissa had found a sense of community at the church and, beyond that, a repose of spirit which she hadn't expected.

Later, she gave Lynn a lesson in how to fry chicken and wasn't surprised that she was an apt pupil. Lynn beamed when they had a taste test, and Nerissa gave her an A-minus.

"Next time I'm getting an A-plus," Lynn declared with flour on her cheek and all over the apron Nerissa had insisted she wear.

Every time the phone rang, Nerissa was on the alert, expecting it to be Helen Reid, but it was invariably for Lynn.

"It's for you," Lynn yelled when Nerissa had given up hope because it was nine p.m.

"I'm sorry to call you so late, Miss Ramsey," Mrs. Reid apologized. "I was having trouble getting in touch with my oldest brother. We'd like you to meet with us tomorrow night at my house. Can you do that?"

"I'd be happy to." The arrangements were made, and Nerissa put the phone down.

Two lessons were to be learned from this, she thought as she glanced at the mirror. Always look your best, and never give up.

"Aunt Rissa. Guess what?" Lynn called as she pelted down the hall. "I'm going home for Thanksgiving. I learned to fry chicken just in time!"

She threw her arms around Nerissa, laughing and crying at the same time as Nerissa held her. "I don't know why I'm crying. I guess it's 'cause I've missed my family so much."

"I know you've been homesick, honey, but you've been very brave, and you've done so well at school. You deserve to see your family." She gave Lynn a tissue for her eyes. "Are you coming back?"

Lynn's eyes opened wide. "Oh yes, Aunt Rissa, I'm going to be The Ghost of Christmas Past. Mrs. Peebles told us we're going to put on the best play the school has ever seen. Ross and I are on the scenery crew, also. They can't do without us."

"You're right, they can't," Nerissa agreed, hugging her niece again.

Monday went by slowly, but at last it was seven o'clock and Nerissa was sitting in Helen Reid's living room. She admired the number of beautiful Oriental pieces, including a large rug. "My late husband was in the Navy and brought something home every trip, so over the years, we accumulated all of this," Mrs. Reid explained.

Gathered around were Mrs. Reid's two sisters, Mary

and Joyce, her two brothers, Charles and Harry, and the aunt's daughter, Millie.

"Millie, why don't you explain to Miss Ramsey about the house?" Mrs. Reid said.

"Mama's been fading for a long time but wouldn't leave her house. Lately she's been falling, and her doctor has finally persuaded her that she can't stay home alone. There's no one who can stay with her, and she refuses to come to my house, so next week she's going to that new place down on Central." Millie seemed to be a gentle but timid woman, Nerissa thought. No wonder her more assertive cousins were helping out.

"May I ask—is it your mother who owns the house?" she asked Millie.

"Yes, and as her only child I have the legal authority to take care of her affairs."

The situation sounded clear enough, and even though Millie came across as meek, she didn't appear unintelligent. So why couldn't she deal with her mother by herself? The answer came immediately.

"Auntie is our mother's only remaining relative, and we're all very close," Mrs. Reid said.

"We need to look out for her interests, you see," said Harry, who was enough like Mrs. Reid to be her twin.

"I do see," Nerissa replied. That was what families did. Looked out for each other.

"Can you tell me what condition the house is in? Are there any major repairs needed?" She looked around the room.

"When was it that we had to put in the new bathroom?" Millie asked.

"About three years ago," Mrs. Reid answered.

"It was painted inside last year," Mary recalled. "Auntie put up a real fuss, but we got it done."

"The outside paint looks to be in good condition," Nerissa observed.

"That was done two years ago," Millie said.

These details made the proposition sound better and better. Of course they hadn't yet mentioned a figure. It was time for her to tell them about herself, so hopefully that could be a positive thing on her side when decision time came.

"I'd like to tell you about my background, so you'll see why I want to rent the house," she began. She was aware that neither Joyce nor Charles had said anything, so she made frequent eye contact with them as she outlined her history and her employment background. She was open about her marriage because she had nothing to hide and she didn't want any of them to hear it later and wonder why she hadn't mentioned it.

"Owning a bookstore, especially one where I can feature resources on black literature, is what I've always wanted to do. I chose Jamison because it seems to be the ideal place as far as I'm concerned. It hasn't been taken over by the big chain stores yet, and it has a number of schools. With hard work, I think such a store could be a success."

"Who do you bank with, Miss Ramsey?" Joyce asked.

"Knowing I was going into business, I set up all my accounts before I left Minneapolis," Nerissa said and named her bank in Jamison.

"That's all well and good," Charles said. His heavy voice and hard glance alerted Nerissa that here was

the dissenting voice she'd expected but had not yet
encountered.

"I've been in business myself a long time, and I know
anyone can have a bank account, even a respectable one
as far as the amount of money in it goes. But my experience tells me that's not enough. I need to know what
kind of reputation a person has locally. Who have you
done business with here? Who knows if you're dependable and honest? Auntie's house can sit empty as far as
I'm concerned until we're sure the person who rents it
is going to take good care of it and pay the bills every
single month and on time. Nothing against you, Miss
Ramsey. That's just good business," he said.

Nerissa was reeling but kept her expression calm.
Everything the man said made good sense. She hadn't
thought of it from that standpoint. Her reputation had
never been questioned. Of course she was dependable
and honest, but there was no one in Jamison who knew
that. She'd only been here two months.

"You're renting where you live, Miss Ramsey?"
Millie asked.

"Yes, I am," she said.

"Where is that?" the gentle voice asked.

"200 Tulip Lane. I rent from Bill Denton."

"Charles, that's DB Enterprises," Mrs. Reid said.

Nerissa was surprised by the instant change in
Charles's attitude.

"DB Enterprises? Well, that puts a different light on
the subject. We can look into it, and maybe we'll have
a tenant after all." While he didn't become genial, the
hard light left his eyes.

Nerissa couldn't leave without asking one more

question. Again she turned to Millie. "In case I am approved, could you tell me when you think the house would be available?"

"Mama's going after Thanksgiving, then we have to clear the house, which will take at least a week. We're in the midst of deciding now who gets what after Mama takes the pieces she wants with her. A round figure might be about the tenth of December, but we'd let you know in writing. Is that all right?"

"Yes, Miss Millie. That's what I need to know."

The meeting was over, and after she left Nerissa went back by the house, circling it twice.

There was no getting away from it. She liked it and craved the opportunity to transform it into the kind of bookstore every reader desired: warm, comfortable, homey, unhurried, and with shelves filled with all sorts of wonderful books that called and enchanted.

The other fact she couldn't get away from was the influence of DB Enterprises.

She had no doubt that had she called them that Monday morning, they would've found a vacancy for her and she'd already be in her bookstore. She wouldn't have had to go through those weeks of searching, felt those depths of discouragement. She would've had the time she needed to get the store stocked and open for the beginning of the Christmas shopping season.

It was humiliating that the only reason Millie's cousin Charles would consider her now was because Bill Denton was her landlord. She'd had to negotiate with him to become his tenant for her residence. She sure didn't want him to have anything to do with her business!

Chapter 17

Tuesday morning Nerissa stayed home waiting for the phone call. All of her thoughts were concentrated on obtaining the blue and white house for her bookstore. When she heard a ring, she picked up the phone, but there was no one there. The ring came again, and she realized it was the doorbell. She signed for a delivery via FedEx that she knew was Lynn's ticket home.

An hour later, the phone rang. It was Mrs. Reid asking if she could come to the Mailroom. Nerissa had to drive carefully on the way so as to not break the speed limit.

"Charlie talked to DB and satisfied himself that you'd be a responsible tenant, Nerissa. The rest of us were already in agreement, so as soon as we move Auntie and clear the house, you can begin with your business." Mrs. Reid named the rental figure, which turned out to be a little higher than Nerissa had hoped for, but would be offset by the good condition of the property. "How does that sound to you?" Her smile seemed to say she was as pleased as Nerissa at the news.

"It sounds wonderful, and I can't thank you enough, Mrs. Reid. I'm going to take good care of the house for you."

The joy that filled her made her smile at the people in

line at the mail counter. Maggie Rose caught her eye and beckoned her over.

"I was going to call you, Nerissa. Chris and I always have an after-Thanksgiving party on Saturday night for our friends. Nothing fancy, just food and fun. You will come, won't you?" There was a hopeful note in her voice.

In her mind, Nerissa put together Chris Shealy and Bill. Bill would certainly be there, but her euphoria didn't permit anything except acceptance.

"I'll be glad to come, Maggie Rose," she said. Nothing could stand in her way now. Not even Bill Denton.

She gave the good news to her dad that night and spent a part of the next day getting Lynn off to Seattle.

Pearline called her that night. "You're not going to spend Thanksgiving alone, Nerissa. Dinner's at four, and I expect to see you here."

Her last three Thanksgivings had been spent alone, so Nerissa was particularly appreciative of the invitation and presented Pearline with red roses when she arrived for dinner.

"Look at that, Harold. Red roses. Now isn't she sweet to do that?"

Pearline found a vase and put the flowers on their own little side table. Nerissa counted ten people at the table, but even so there was enough food to go around, and when she went home, Pearline insisted on her taking some leftover turkey with all its fixings and pumpkin pie.

"So you won't have to cook while Lynn's gone," she said.

***

Thanksgiving at the senior Dentons was always a big family affair. People stayed in their own homes on Christmas and then visited around, but everyone ate together for Thanksgiving.

Bill was in his element. He stood at the butcher block table in the kitchen while he carved the twenty-two pound turkey that was his contribution to the dinner.

The house was crammed with family, and the noise was sometimes deafening as the children played and the music on the CD player was turned up louder. The platters were finally piled high and placed on the table with the rest of the food. Everyone sat, grace was said by his father, and the meal began.

Bill rarely missed this Thanksgiving ritual. It was important to him as a reaffirmation of family and his place in it. Here he was secure and loved. He had a place of his own.

He took part in the conversation, passed food back and forth, enjoyed the savory dishes, and watched the children in their playful bickering as they tried to see who could outeat the other.

Then a strange thing happened. There was silence around him, and although he could see the children's mouths moving, he heard nothing.

In some hidden recess of his being, he was only aware that none of these children belonged to him. Where was his son? His little girl? Where was the woman who would give him these children and be the other half of him for the rest of his life?

"Bill, wake up. Pass the dressing." Dan nudged him.

"Sorry, guess I didn't hear you," Bill said and passed the dish. He felt Dan's curious glance and wasn't surprised when he muttered, "I want to talk to you later."

But he didn't want to talk with Dan or anyone. After dinner was over, he waited until Dan was in the kitchen, then slipped away.

The clear, starry night was perfect for the mood he was in. He drove into Charleston and stopped at Waterfront Park. He was not alone as he strolled slowly through the park, gazing at Charleston Harbor. A surprising number of people had apparently decided this was the thing to do after their Thanksgiving dinner.

When he'd gone off into that fog, as Dan called it, and thought about children, his children, he'd been astonished. That was such an odd thing to do, downright peculiar. He liked kids, always had, got along with them fine. He had fun with Yvonne's Becky and Matthew. Never had a problem with children like Breia and Josie at his studio. But until now, having his own hadn't been a significant part of his thinking.

To be honest, he didn't want it to be now because the implications were too great. He wasn't ready to tackle them.

He turned around and walked back to his car. Perhaps these were the kinds of thoughts you began having when you turned thirty-five, which was only a few months away for him.

On Friday, Bill was returning from a photo shoot when he saw a familiar pickup in front of him. It was Nerissa, distinctive in her posture and the angle of her head. He followed her without thinking, hoping for the courage to speak to her if she stopped.

She turned off Main Street, went down to the corner where the restaurant was and turned, parking across the street. Good. Maybe he could persuade her to have a meal with him. He parked behind her and got out, swiftly calculating that it had been nearly three weeks since she got so angry at him. Maybe time had done its work and she wasn't so mad now.

He was at her door to open it for her.

"Hi. Nerissa. I'm so glad to see you. . . . I'm going to ask you straight out, are you still mad at me?"

He could tell she'd been surprised to see him and that his question had caught her off guard. That was a hopeful sign.

"Not as much as I was," she said, giving him a straight look that was a warning not to mess with her.

He couldn't help his big smile. "Thank God! Before another word, please let me apologize for being so flat-out stupid. I hope to never do something like that again. Have you found a place for your bookstore?"

Why was she looking at him in disbelief? Had he messed up again, unbeknownst to him?

"Don't you know?" she asked.

"Nerissa, I wouldn't be asking you if I knew," he said patiently.

"I'm renting this house." She indicated the blue and white residence.

"I thought Millie's mother lived here," he said.

"She's going to an assisted living facility in a few days."

"I haven't been in the place for a few years," he said, "but I know Millie and her cousins keep it up to par." He was glad for her sake that her search was over, but mostly he was drinking her in after a long dry spell. She looked great in her black denims and long red jacket, her skin slightly flushed by the cool wind and her hair loose without the headscarf he was used to seeing.

She looked a little uncertain. "Were you following me?" she asked.

"Yes. I noticed your pickup in front of me and I needed to speak to you. I hope you don't mind. In fact, when you turned in here, I thought you were going to the restaurant and I wanted to see if we could have a meal together. Could we, Nerissa?"

He saw a little warmth come into her eyes and it was all he could do not to reach for her. Slow, he warned himself. *Go slow!*

"I can't, Bill," she said.

"Another time?" he asked.

"I'm up to my ears in planning right now," she explained.

"I understand. Will you allow me to help, Nerissa?" This was vitally important to him. He couldn't let another long period separate them.

She gave him a considering stare, and he knew he was being measured. He prayed she'd not find him wanting.

She smiled. "I can probably find something you can do. Thanks for the offer."

He couldn't restrain himself from touching her hand. "Thanks, Nerissa. I'll see you later."

He hurried away before she could change her mind.

Chapter 18

Her unexpected meeting with Bill had added to the adrenaline that had been fueling Nerissa since getting the blue and white house. She'd scarcely been able to sleep, but she made herself eat. Her figure was filling out a little, chasing away the gaunt aspect her mirror had shown her not so long ago.

Bill's appearance had utterly surprised her. He looked so handsome, so familiar, that it caught her breath.

He apologized and she had to accept it. She had questioned his honesty based on one incident, just as Mrs. Reid's brother had questioned hers based on nothing at all.

The misunderstanding between them had been emotional baggage that she didn't need, especially now when things were finally going right. At first she'd had a niggling suspicion that he'd had a hand in her getting Millie's mother's house, but he hadn't known anything about it. The air was clear between them now and she was glad.

So glad that when she went home, she went right to her closet. He would certainly be at the party tomorrow night, and she intended to look her best. While working in the library she'd accumulated a variety of pants and separates because they were comfortable and fitted her tall figure. She almost decided on one of her favorites, then turned to the other end of the closet.

She wanted to wear a dress. She wanted to feel feminine and sexy like Jan. But in her own style.

When she arrived at the Shealy house the next night, the party was well under way, judging by the light spilling out of the windows, the sounds of laughter, and the number of cars parked in the cleared section. She looked for Bill's Mercedes but didn't see it. Her heart sank a little. Probably he was just late.

Maggie Rose welcomed her and introduced her husband, whom Nerissa had not met when she went to the ranch. Chris had an angular face and deep-set eyes with dark brows. He had an aura of competence and authority. Nerissa could see why HS Stables was so successful.

"Sorry I was busy when you were here before," he said. "We're so glad you could come tonight. Let me introduce you to some of our other friends." She met five or six people, then Maggie Rose captured her and took her to the kitchen.

"You'll meet everyone sooner or later without introductions. It's more fun that way. Let me get you something to drink and then you can tell me what you did for Thanksgiving."

Nerissa leaned against the counter relaxing and exchanging Thanksgiving dinner stories with Maggie Rose. She'd turned to set her glass down when she heard Bill's voice. "Maggie Rose, I saw a pickup in the yard that looks . . ." Nerissa turned around slowly, and Bill drew in his breath.

Neither of them noticed Maggie Rose, who picked up a tray of canapes and left the room.

Nerissa was wearing a black dress with a shirred crossover neckline. The silk crepe lovingly followed the supple lines of her figure. Her only jewelry was a silver necklace and matching earrings. Sheer hose and black strappy slingbacks with two-inch heels completed the outfit. She'd put on a touch of eye makeup and curled her hair.

It was worth it. Bill's gaze was so intense, she felt heat rising in her face.

He cleared his throat. "You are absolutely stunning, Nerissa." His voice was low and husky. "I didn't know you were coming. We could have come together."

"I wasn't sure what your plans were," she said, her gaze locked with his.

Bill started moving toward her. "Nerissa," he said, his voice honey-sweet to her ears. She knew she should move, but she couldn't.

As he reached for her, Chris came through the door. "Bill. Where have you—" He stopped. "Excuse me," he said as he backed out.

"We need to go into the other room," Nerissa said.

"It was only Chris," Bill protested.

"It'll be someone else next time. Kitchens are busy places at parties, you know." She was trying to slow her pulse while secretly wishing Chris had come along several minutes later.

She linked her hand in his. "I've only met a few people. You can tell me who the rest are."

"I'm not sure I want the other guys to meet you," he growled. "But I guess we can't hide out here all evening, even though that's what I want to do."

Nerissa was aware of curious glances as they came

into the dining room, where people were gathered around the table, filling their plates with crab cakes, deviled eggs, riblets, potato salad, fried shrimp, red rice, and other delicacies. On a smaller table was a variety of desserts, and as she and Bill began to circulate with their plates, she was struck again by the casual bounty of Southern hospitality. Minneapolis was never like this.

It seemed everyone took their food and crowded into the living room so as not to miss anything. Nerissa was amused at the manner in which Bill co-opted a narrow loveseat for the two of them. When the man who'd been sitting in it returned, "Bill said, "Sorry, Jim. If you move, you lose."

"Introduce me to the lady, Bill, and I won't complain." He grinned and stuck out his hand as Bill said, "Nerissa Ramsey, Jim Phillips." Then he added, "Jim's the best carpenter around and might be able to help you when you're ready."

"Ready with what?" Jim found a place on the floor next to the loveseat.

"Transforming a house into a bookstore," Nerissa said.

"What kind of bookstore?" the woman next to Jim asked.

As she answered the question and the ones that followed, Nerissa was acutely aware that these were Bill's friends. People he grew up with, had gone to school with. Their conversation was full of tags and references to events she couldn't share. Yet he hadn't brought a date with him as he surely must have done in past years.

The way he was acting in keeping her near him probably made his friends think she was his date. She didn't know about the men, but she was sure the women saw their age difference. What they thought of it, she didn't know. She didn't even know what Chris, his closest friend, thought.

A good-looking woman across the room, who'd tried to engage Bill's attention in the dining room, said, "Have you been in business before?"

"No, I haven't," Nerissa answered.

"Then how do you expect to succeed?" she asked unsmilingly.

Nerissa recognized a challenge. She straightened her shoulders and lifted her chin. Reminding herself these were Bill's friends, she replied in her most gracious manner that she'd been head librarian at a college, so she knew the business side. Here in Jamison she hoped to find out from teachers and other readers the kinds of books they wanted but had trouble finding, especially books by and about blacks. That was a niche she planned to fill, and she'd appreciate anyone's input.

She felt Bill's fingers bestow a fleeting caress on the back of her neck as Chris announced that coffee was ready to go with the desserts.

In the general movement toward the dining room, Jerlene, Maggie Rose's sister, pulled Nerissa aside.

"Maybe you can help me," she said. Nerissa had noticed earlier that while Maggie Rose had an air of tranquility about her, Jerlene seemed to be filled with energy and movement. "Come sit down here with me," she said, taking Nerissa's hand and guiding her to a corner. "Bill can spare you for a minute." She directed a mischievous glance at him.

"Seriously, I need help with my twelve-year-old son,

Covey. His dad and I can't seem to do anything to get him to read. But we don't know a lot about what books are out there for a kid like him."

"What is he interested in?" This was always the first question Nerissa asked.

"Horses and anything to do with them, but he doesn't like to read."

"If you can get him in the bookstore, I can guarantee to find a book he'll want to read," Nerissa said confidently. "I intend to set aside a whole room for youngsters like him. Reading is the foundation of an education that will help our kids toward success in life, and the way to do that for reluctant readers is to entice them with good stories. I know it can be done, Jerlene." Nerissa had to stop herself before going on and on about her passion.

"All my nine-year-old wants to do is draw pictures," a man who had stood listening to them said. "I'll bring him in for you to find him a book too."

Another couple engaged Nerissa in conversation about living in Minneapolis, and by the time she'd managed to get herself a piece of pecan pie and coffee, Jim Phillips was at her side.

"Come sit here," he invited, pulling out a chair for her. "So how do you like Jamison?" he asked.

In a swift glance around the room, Nerissa located Bill laughing with a group of people. The woman who'd asked her about running a business stood close to him.

Nerissa gave her full attention to Jim as they talked about Jamison and other places. A slim man who looked familiar introduced himself. "I'm Hugh Peebles, Lucy's cousin. You impressed her, and I can see why." He paid the compliment lightly as he pulled up a nearby chair, but she saw admiration in his eyes.

So this was how it felt, she thought, having men vie for her attention. Before Ric, she'd been busy with home, work, and school and unsure of herself when it came to socializing with men. She was too tall and too plain. She'd wondered how girls like Jan sparkled so easily with their male companions. But she was getting the hang of it, and it was fun.

Especially since Bill was enjoying himself with that woman.

She'd been aware all evening of soft music, but now a rocking instrumental with a strong beat came on.

"Let's dance, Nerissa," Jim said, taking her hand and leading her to the dining room with its hardwood floor. The table had been moved into a corner and the lights turned low.

Other people were already on the floor, moving, laughing, competing with each other and filling the air with rhythmic vitality. Nerissa was caught up in it, and although she hadn't danced in years, she let herself simply respond to the music. Hugh claimed her next, challenging her to learn a new step.

The slow blues came on, and she found herself in Bill's arms.

"Hello," he said softly, holding her close to him.

"Hello, yourself," she replied just as softly. Then she let her eyelids close and gave in to her body's desire to follow with Bill wherever the music led.

After the dancing, people began to drift away. When Nerissa went into the kitchen to help with the dishes, Maggie Rose said, "Don't bother with these now,

Nerissa. Chris and I want you to stay after the others have left, so don't run away."

Jerlene and her husband, Matt, were the last to leave. "Don't forget about books for Covey," Jerlene reminded Nerissa.

Chris closed the door and looked around the room with a sigh.

"How you feeling?" Bill asked Nerissa.

"Fine. I was in the kitchen and Maggie Rose chased me out, but I'm going back in." She flicked him a questioning glance.

"I'm in." He shucked his jacket and began rolling up his sleeves.

"I didn't ask you to stay to clean up," Maggie Rose protested.

Chris placed her in a chair in the kitchen, removed her shoes and put her feet on a hassock. "All you have to do is supervise."

The next hour was almost as pleasant for Nerissa as the party had been. She had never done this kind of thing with Ric. Even when their marriage had been new, he never was part of such activity. He seemed to think it was beneath him.

She loved the camaraderie, the easy way Chris and Maggie Rose accepted her. Chris, following Maggie Rose's directions, dealt with the food, then began setting the furniture to rights while she and Bill washed dishes and cleaned the kitchen as though they'd worked together for years.

She was thankful for Maggie Rose's presence because she and Bill seemed to touch each other frequently at the sink or catch each other's gaze. The current between them was there again, wordless but compelling.

After everything was back in order, Chris put Maggie Rose on the couch with pillows behind her back and her legs outstretched. "That feels sooo good," she said with a sigh.

"We should really go," Nerissa said. "You and the baby need rest."

"Don't you dare leave. You have to rest, too, and have at least one cup of freshly made coffee, which Chris is fixing, and how about another dessert?"

"You heard the lady." Bill gently tugged Nerissa down beside him on the love seat but didn't release her hand. "Did you wash away your pretty nail polish?"

She didn't realize he'd even noticed. "It's still there," she said, her head close to his.

He turned his face and holding her eyes, brought her fingers to his lips. She felt the kiss in her throat, and the heat of it reflected in her face. Had Maggie Rose seen it? When she looked up, Maggie Rose was watching Chris coming from the kitchen with coffee and pie.

Nerissa looked around the large, comfortable room and then at the couch, where Chris settled down with Maggie Rose's feet in his lap. He was massaging them with one hand while drinking coffee with the other. Maggie Rose looked blissfully content. Bill, gently stroking her hand, was talking with Chris.

There was nothing quiet or contented in the way she felt. She was wound up, her heart fluttering, wondering what was going to happen once she and Bill left the safety of this room. She could sense tension in Bill as well.

When she couldn't stand it any longer, she set her cup aside. "I really must be going. It's been a great evening."

Bill was beside her in an instant, and she found herself out the door and on the way to her pickup in a matter of minutes.

"I hate that I can't drive you home," Bill complained.

"I give you permission this time to follow me," she said and smiled up at him.

"Don't worry, I'll be right behind you," he promised.

At Tulip Lane, he pulled in front of her. By the time she parked, he was there to help her from the truck. He walked her to her door.

"May I come in?"

"Yes," she said and handed him her key.

They stepped inside. He closed the door and gave her back the key.

"Now," he said, holding her face between his palms and brushing her lips, her cheeks and her closed eyelids with feather touches.

She opened her eyes in surprise to see a sweet smile on his face. "I've been wanting to do that so long," he murmured.

"And this." He slipped one hand behind her head and kissed her again.

She was drowning in the thrilling sensations. It was wrong, she shouldn't be doing this, and she was going to regret it.

"Meow." The sudden sound startled her.

Bill broke his kiss, and they looked down. The cat was twining itself around his legs.

"Go away, cat," he growled.

"Bill." She was thankful Beans had brought her to her

senses. She was shaken. How long had it been since she'd felt passion? "We'd better say good night."

"Shhhh," he said. "I'm just catching my breath."

She stood perfectly still, trying to subdue the pulsing of her nerves. Bill again held her face in his palms and kissed her lightly.

"Good night, sweet Nerissa."

Nerissa heard his feet cross the porch and go down the steps. Then she turned out the lamp and went into her bedroom, where she sat in her chair, fully dressed, and pondered her dilemma.

Chapter 19

"Good morning. Sleep well?"

The nine-thirty phone call from Bill on Sunday morning surprised Nerissa as she was drinking her second cup of coffee.

"Morning, Bill. Yes, I did. How about you?" That wasn't strictly true as she had tossed and turned, alternately delighting in the memory of Bill's kisses and despairing at how to control her desire for more.

"Took me a long time to get to sleep. I kept thinking about you and how much I enjoyed our time together." The warmth in his voice went right through her.

"It was a lovely evening," she said. "I hadn't danced in such a long time, I didn't know if I still could," she confessed, a smile in her voice.

"Trust me, honey, you can," he asserted. "I'd love to take you dancing some night. Have you been to any of the clubs here?"

"No, I haven't." She didn't want to pursue this. It would only get her deeper into wanting his company, and she couldn't afford to do that.

"I'll put that on a later agenda. I called to see if I could take you to breakfast."

"Thanks, Bill, but I've already had breakfast and I'm getting ready to go to church."

"How about dinner, then?"

"I can't, Bill, but thanks. I'm swamped with work to do now that I have the store." She stirred her cold coffee, hoping he wasn't offended, but she had to protect herself and she really did have work to do.

"Even on a Sunday evening?" He didn't sound convinced.

"You're in business, Bill, and you frequently work on Sundays, don't you?"

"Yeah, I guess you're right. I won't press you this time. You're going to be busy, I know, but Nerissa?"

"Yes?"

"Don't forget me." There was almost a warning in his words.

"That'd be hard to do," she said lightly. "After all, you are next door." But as the conversation ended, she was sure that he was thinking, as was she, that they'd both effectively ignored each other these past weeks even though they were only a driveway apart.

She drove to church with two goals in mind. To give thanks for finding the store and to discipline herself where Bill Denton was concerned.

She was unwilling to trust her emotions to him because she was afraid to open herself to pain again. Last night, she'd felt life flowing through her once more for the first time in three years. It had been exhilarating—and frightening—because if she gave into it entirely, it would sweep her away. And if the relationship failed, if Bill found her inadequate as a woman and she ended up as she had with Ric, she'd not be able to endure it. So better to nip it in the bud. Now. Today.

The words of the sermon poured over her, but she was so focused on her internal task, she hardly heard them.

Afterwards Lucy Peebles came up to her. "I hear you have your store. How do you like it?"

"It's going to be good because it's a house. Can you come over and look at it? I've some ideas about how to use the rooms and I'd appreciate your thoughts," Nerissa said.

"I'm out of school about three p.m. most days, but how about this coming Saturday? Is that too soon?"

After they made the arrangements, Lucy said, "My cousin called me first thing this morning raving about you, Nerissa. You certainly made an impression on him at the party last night." She smiled broadly.

Nerissa was blank for a moment, then remembered the familiar-looking man who said his name was Hugh Peebles.

"You can't be serious," she told Lucy. "All we did was talk a little and danced once."

"It must have been enough for him," Lucy said. "Anyway, I'll see you on Saturday."

Nerissa worked hard in her office the rest of the day until the time came to pick up Lynn at the airport. The plane was delayed, which gave her time to look over a Sunday paper someone had thrown down in the next seat. The fashion section had a feature about gowns for the upcoming holiday season, which reminded Nerissa of her black dress. She had only that one. This one in the ad, with its low neckline and a side slit, looked quite appealing.

Nerissa smiled. If Hugh Peebles or Jim Phillips wanted to take her dancing, she could wear this with ease and enjoy the dancing for its own sake. No complications because there'd be no emotions. Just fun and *laughter*. She looked at the dress wistfully. If only life were that simple.

Lynn arrived wearing a new jacket and carrying a gift-wrapped box. "This is for you from Mom and Dad, and I've got so much to tell you," she began.

The telling lasted all the way home, interspersed with questions about Nerissa's Thanksgiving. As they pulled into the driveway, Lynn asked, "Did you see Mr. Bill while I was gone?"

"As a matter of fact, I did. We happened to both go to a party at the HS Stables."

"I'm glad. I'd sure like to go out there again myself. Maybe take some lessons. Do you think I could, Aunt Rissa?" In the house Lynn hurried into her room, threw off her jacket, and filled her arms with her stuffed toys.

Nerissa opened her box and pulled out a long, cream-colored cashmere scarf. It was soft and warm around her neck. "It's lovely," she said.

"I told Mom you'd like it because it'll go well with your black and brown outfits." She laid her animals down. "Aunt Rissa, thank you for letting me live here with you. I couldn't wait to get back yesterday," she said. She stood almost stiffly in front of Nerissa.

"Didn't you have a good time at home?" Nerissa asked, putting her arms loosely around Lynn's shoulders, hoping she would relax.

"Seeing my family when everyone came for Thanksgiving was great. Talking with Mom and Dad and

Grace, I loved that." She was speaking slowly, Nerissa thought, as she analyzed her feelings. "Friday we all went shopping, but by Saturday I began to think of the Christmas play and Ross and Keisha and you. I like it here and how you treat me, Aunt Rissa." She threw her arms around Nerissa, who hugged her back, thankful for the insight Lynn was developing.

On Monday Nerissa had her first look inside the blue and white house. The front door led into a hall with two rooms on each side. At the back of the house were the kitchen, bathroom, and laundry room. It was an old structure, so the bedrooms had only small closets. She wouldn't be able to see the true condition of the walls until all of the furniture was gone, but they seemed to be clean.

"We moved Mama to her new place Saturday. We decided we can be out of here sooner; so you can take possession as of Sunday, December fifth. If that suits you, we can take care of the rental agreement now," Millie said.

As soon as that was done, Nerissa rushed home and called her suppliers, filling them in on her accomplishment and giving them an initial order.

Now she could relax and plan a design for the inside of the house.

Chris Shealy was still dismissing his last student when Bill arrived, so Bill passed the time of day with Tallie Sims. Chris had inherited him when Chris's uncle died. He lived with Chris and Maggie Rose, who considered him irreplaceable as a horseman and friend.

"You doing okay, Mr. Tallie?" he asked, shading his eyes against the sunset.

"Sure am. How 'bout you? Don't see near as much of you as I used to." Bill didn't know how old Mr. Tallie was. Had to be at least in his seventies, yet his skin was still smooth over his thin face. Never had carried much weight, although he liked to cook. They exchanged recipes once in a while.

"Chris has Maggie Rose now. Married men don't hang out with single men much. At least they shouldn't," Bill said.

"Shouldn't what?" Chris asked, coming up beside Bill.

Bill repeated what he'd said.

"Doesn't mean you have to be such a stranger," Mr. Tallie said as he went over the stable.

"He's right, you know. Now I've got to call you to get you out here." Chris clapped Bill on the shoulder. "Don't stay away."

Bill felt relief and realized for the first time that he'd subconsciously put a restraint on seeing Chris because he was now married. It'd been hard because he and Chris shared memories and confidences that even Bill's brothers knew nothing about.

He cuffed Chris on the arm. "Am I here just so you can jump on me?" He grinned.

"I had to do that first, but I have a job for you also. The Christmas holidays are coming up, and I want to do an ad to persuade parents that a series of six lessons would be a great gift to put under the tree for their youngsters."

"Why limit it to kids?"

"They're the ones out of school for at least two

weeks, longer for some college students," Chris said thoughtfully.

"How about a lineup of all five of your horses, each with a rider of a definite age group?" Bill suggested.

"When can you do it?" Chris asked.

"You get the people lined up and call me."

"Come on in the office while I look at some files," Chris said.

It had been a while since Bill had been inside, and as he looked at the large schedule by Maggie Rose's desk, surprise made him say, "Man! You've got every space filled now."

"Yeah. Great, isn't it? Remember when I had time to work on that other job?"

"So how come you're running an ad? There's no hours in the day for you to handle more students."

"Some of my regular students will be away for the holidays. The new ones will take their places. People take their kids out when money runs tight or the child doesn't want to come anymore, so the only way to keep that roster full is to advertise." He found the files he was looking for under a stack on the desk and asked, "Coffee or soda?"

"Coffee, of course."

When they were seated, coffee in hand, Chris said, "I must have missed something here. One week you told us about this tall lady with green eyes who'd talked you into letting her rent your place and fix it up. Maggie Rose sees her in the Mailroom and says she's not someone you'd forget. She brings her niece and another kid here for some school report and I don't even get a peek at her, but Maggie Rose wants to invite her to the party, so we do. Next thing I know, I walk into my kitchen and there's this stunner with long legs, curvy dress, and green eyes looking like a rabbit caught in headlights and you advancing on her like the wolf that wants to devour her."

Chris's fanciful description had Bill laughing so hard he had to hold his cup with both hands.

Chris had to chuckle at his own description. "That was pretty good, wasn't it? Seriously, Bill, what gives with the lovely Nerissa?"

Bill gave Chris a brief factual account of Nerissa and the house, of Jan and Lynn, the movie date, and the resemblance between him and Nerissa's ex-husband in Minneapolis that Lynn and Jan had mentioned.

"Has Nerissa said anything about her ex?" Chris nursed his cup, keeping his hands warm.

"Not one word. Never discusses her background except as a librarian."

"Have you asked her?" He raised his eyebrows at Bill.

Bill shook his head. Chris waited, sipping his coffee.

"What you have to understand is that Nerissa is very smart, and extremely independent. From our first words to one another, she was battling me, and of course I fought back. I'd no idea I reminded her of her ex. All I knew was I couldn't say anything right. I let her have the house because she insisted, but I thought she'd fail and that would be the end of it."

"She proved you wrong," Chris said, getting up to refill the cups.

"Did she ever! Wait 'til you see the house and the yard. She's very private about her affairs and actually, our time at the party is the longest we've ever spent together. And without arguing."

Chris looked at Bill and shook his head.

"What?" Bill asked.

"For two guys who've been best friends all our lives, we sure are different. I've known Maggie Rose since she was nine years old and she was always the one for me. You, on the other hand, met Nerissa—how long ago?"

"End of September."

"And this is the end of November, two months."

"It probably doesn't make sense, Chris. But there's something about her that makes other women I've known pale by comparison. Know what I mean?"

Chris nodded. "Those years Maggie Rose was in Connecticut, I ran around but I could never get serious, not as long as she was free. How does Nerissa feel about you?" he asked.

"I know there's something between us. She knows it too, but she's fighting it every step of the way."

Chris chuckled. "Didn't seem to be fighting it Saturday night." After a silence, he asked, "So now what?"

"I'm not giving up, but I'll have to go slow. Can't push her or she'll—"

"Bolt," Chris concluded, "like a thoroughbred who has to get used to a gentle but firm hand."

"She might not like it, but that's not a bad analogy since I call her Miss High-and-Mighty." Bill smiled reminiscently.

"So you've decided you're going to see this one through, Bill? All the way?" Chris's eyes were serious.

Bill understood the reference. Before he'd always walked away if the affair lasted too long.

"Can't walk away from Nerissa, Chris. I'm in for the long haul."

"Then I wish you the best of luck, buddy. Call if I can help."

He'd probably need all kinds of help, Bill mused, but not the kind Chris could provide.

Chapter 20

Nerissa found it was hard to stay away from a man and pretend indifference when he lived next door and anytime she went outdoors, she ran the risk of seeing him. How had she managed it before when she was angry at him? It must have been that he was avoiding her as well.

But no more. Monday and Tuesday he was coming down his steps as she pulled out of her driveway, and they'd waved at each other. This evening they'd arrived home at the same time, and he came across to her.

"How're things going?" he asked as she stepped out of the pickup.

"Good. I've signed the lease." She had to smile when she said that. It was still such great news after those days of discouragement.

Bill reached into the back and lifted out the grocery bags. "Sounds to me like that calls for a celebration." He followed her to the porch.

"Come in for a moment," she said as she opened the door.

He placed the bags on the kitchen counter. "You ready to go out and celebrate?" He repeated his invitation, his eyes on hers.

She led the way back to the living room, and although it wasn't polite not to ask him to sit down, she couldn't risk it. She jammed her hands in her jacket pockets. "The only celebrating I'm doing right now has to do with getting the store ready. My goal is to open it before Christmas."

He whistled softly. "That's a tight schedule. You'll be pushing yourself very hard," he said with concern.

She lifted her chin as she met his eyes. "That was always my goal, and despite the setback of not finding a place right away, I still intend to reach it." She didn't mean to be argumentative, it was just a statement of fact, and she hoped her voice conveyed that.

He continued his searching gaze. "Okay. Just try to be careful and don't forget to eat and sleep. All right?"

Nerissa drew in a breath. She really did not want to fight with Bill, especially when his objective was her well-being.

"I'll try," she said, feeling the current between them again. She knew she should not have invited him in, but how could she not when he'd had her groceries? She was convinced he felt it also when the look in his eyes softened and he caressed her cheek with his finger.

She searched for a subject to break the flow. "Lynn came back Sunday night."

He blinked his eyes. "She enjoy herself?"

"She said she did until Saturday. Then she started missing people here."

"I'm not surprised. That reminds me, Ross seems to like her quite a bit. Says she's fun and interesting." He glanced into the other room. "Is she home?"

"She's here. I left her doing homework while I ran to the store."

"Then I'd better be going," he said, his hand on the doorknob.

"I've been wanting to tell you how glad I am you're going to Nova Scotia, Bill. When will you know more about the travel arrangements?"

"She said within six weeks, which means before the end of this month."

"Got your bags packed?"

"Sure have. December's a big month for both of us, Nerissa," he murmured.

He was going to kiss her. "Yes, it is." She took a step back, but she couldn't resist touching him. She put a finger on his cheek and said, "I wish us both good luck."

If you played with fire you got burnt, she thought, hanging up her jacket after Bill left. He'd held her finger to his cheek, then pressed a kiss on the palm of the same hand. *One way or another,* his message had been, *you will be kissed*!

It was a good thing he wouldn't hear from Nova Scotia until the end of the month, Bill thought, as he worked in his studio. People who hadn't had a studio photo all year suddenly wanted one to send out with Christmas greetings on it.

A few thoughtful folks had theirs taken in November, but most waited for early December. He always tried to accommodate everyone, telling the late, late ones that the card could be sent after Christmas with a small change in the wording.

Yesterday, he had a four-generational group of twenty-one, and it had taken him a long time to get the photo he wanted. The studio, he realized, was becoming too small for him. It was time to plan for a bigger place, somewhere downtown.

A call from Dan interrupted him.

"You ran out on me Thanksgiving. I told you I wanted to talk," he said.

"I didn't see you when I was ready to leave," Bill fudged. "What's up?"

"What's up with you? You went off into a deep fog right at the table. You having problems, Bro?"

"Nothing that time won't solve. Like when do they want me in Nova Scotia and when will people get their Christmas card photographs done on time so I'm not swamped."

Dan was not convinced. "What's happening with you and Nerissa?"

"I've apologized and we're talking again. In fact, I just saw her tonight. She found a rental and expects to open her store before Christmas."

He gave Dan the details and Dan seemed to be satisfied. "Don't mess up again," he said.

Nerissa had decided that the paint on the outside of the bookstore was good enough for now, which meant money and time for more immediate needs. She'd begin by painting all the woodwork inside. Bookshelves would cover ninety-five percent of the inside walls, leaving only the bathroom and laundry room to consider. Jim Phillips came and they went from room to room, excusing themselves to the movers, measuring for shelves.

She knew that once the books arrived, pricing and shelving them, arranging displays, and adding the individual touches that would entice customers would take the most time. So she allotted minimal time for these basic tasks.

She put ads in the Jamison and Charleston papers about the grand opening on Sunday, December nineteenth, which gave her six shopping days before Christmas. On her list she also had electrician, cash registers, lighting, total insurance coverage, furniture, and office equipment.

Lynn, Ross, and Keisha were invaluable. Lucy came when she could and recommended a high school senior named Gerard as a clerical assistant who was smart and responsible. Millie had a man clean the yard of all debris so cars could park in it.

The days passed by in a blur. One night she was in the store looking at a box of books she'd opened when Bill knocked on the window.

"Come in out of the cold," she said. The weather had turned chilly the night before, and she'd responded by wearing woolen pants, a heavy sweater, and boots. She saw Bill had done the same.

"I brought you something." He handed her a basket.

"It smells marvelous," she said. "You're so thoughtful, Bill. Thanks."

"When was the last time you sat down to eat a full meal?" he asked.

"I'm not sure, but I'm going to right now." She sat on the floor, her back against a wall and patted the floor beside her. Together they took roast chicken, rice, corn pudding, and greens from the basket plus plates, napkins, silverware, and rolls.

"I know this didn't come from any restaurant," Nerissa said, taking her first bite of tender meat.

"You're right. I got it from my mom," he said.

"Bless her heart for cooking it, and bless yours for bringing it."

Nerissa ate slowly, savoring every bite and realizing how much she'd missed this simple pleasure.

He asked questions about the store, and she answered them. "I'll give you a tour when dinner's over," she promised.

"There's pie and a thermos of coffee," he said when their plates were empty. "You want it now or later?"

"I don't think I can eat another bite right now. Your mother's cooking is too good."

"I'm staying to help with whatever you're doing, so dessert can wait."

She didn't think that was a good idea as far as her emotions were concerned, but what could she do? Maybe she'd steal this quiet time with him to hold in her memory.

"I imagine you're busy this time of the year," she said, turning her face toward him.

"Very busy. That's why I haven't been here sooner."

She looked at him closely. "You look tired. Now I can tell *you* about doing too much," she said, but her voice was gentle.

She expected him to smile, but his expression remained drawn.

"What is it, Bill?" she asked.

"Do you remember my story about Mrs. Martin, who

wanted a picnic photograph? I learned that she died last night. One of her daughters called me."

She put her hand on his. "I'm sorry, Bill. The hospice nurse was right about her not having much time. The family will always cherish that photo."

"I hope so." He sighed. "I'm not sure why I'm sad. Maybe it's because I've been thinking of families lately and visiting my mom and dad every week," he reflected. "Your parents living, Nerissa?" He turned his body to her.

"My dad's living with my sisters in Seattle, but my mother died when I was eighteen. Someone like Mrs. Martin always makes me remember."

"I didn't mean to make you sad, too," he said.

"I was just beginning college, but I lived at home, which was good because Alice and Jan were still little girls. Dad never remarried, so between us we raised them."

"Was it terribly hard?" he asked, his eyes never leaving her face.

"It seemed like it at times, but looking back I can see they didn't give me nearly as much trouble as young kids do now."

"But it must have taken all your time."

"I never went out socially anyway because I needed good grades to get and keep scholarships."

He wanted Nerissa to tell him about Ric, and she might as well, she thought. There would never be a better time.

"I began working in the library system as soon as I got out of college, and after some years, met Ric, who was also in the system. We were married a little over four years, then divorced. I worked another three years, then came here."

Please don't ask me why we divorced. I can't bear to have you know.

"Thank you for telling me, Nerissa." He put his arm around her and laid her head on his chest. "You've been through some tough times, but you've come out on top. As far as I'm concerned, you're a class act, Ms. Ramsey."

Nerissa wanted to tell him he was classy too, for simply accepting her story and not pressing for intimate details.

Later, as he helped her shelve the books and they had their dessert and coffee, she noticed the absence of the usual current of awareness between them.

Was it because they were both tired and a little subdued, or was it because something about her history bothered Bill?

Chapter 21

The rain was coming down in torrents.

Nerissa listened to it disbelievingly. Not today. Not for the grand opening of her Book Boutique!

The last four days had been chilly but clear. She hadn't heard anything about approaching bad weather, so maybe it was a swiftly passing shower.

"Is it supposed to rain all day?" she asked Lynn and Ross, who were shifting books in the stock room.

"Gosh, I hope not, Aunt Rissa, because it'll keep people away for sure." Her mouth drooped, then her usual smile appeared. "But it's only ten o'clock and we don't open 'til one, so I bet it'll stop by then."

"People who want to get those discounts you advertised will come," Ross said with certainty.

"I got my mom and some of her friends to promise to come, rain or shine, and they're coming right after church," Keisha said. "So don't worry, Miss Rissa."

"My team," Nerissa said affectionately.

A little later Gerard arrived to get more practice on the cash register. A senior in high school, he'd been recommended by Lucy as smart and dependable. At noon Nerissa sent them all out to get lunch, warning them to be back in forty-five minutes.

She went from room to room, beginning at the front door, looking at the place the way a newcomer would see it. The first impression was of brightness and light. In the room on the right, the office, the first thing that caught the eye were three large bouquets placed along the countertop. She'd purchased one herself; the other two were unexpected congratulatory tokens from her family and from Bill Denton. The shelves carried new publications.

The next room held books on history, science, and social sciences with a table and chair in the corner. Across the hall was fiction and the arts, while the room across from the office had a banner that said, "For our youthful readers."

In each room there was still space on the shelves, which would be filled gradually, but she was glad to have a good representation of books in such a short time. Chairs were scattered here and there as space permitted. She'd had to remind herself over and over that this was a commercial enterprise, not a place for people to browse for hours and depart without buying a book. Still, it was important to have a welcoming atmosphere.

Her initial thought for today was to have cookies and punch, but again had decided no since fingers dusted with cookie crumbs would damage the books. But there were gaily colored posters of characters in children's books and author prints in the other rooms. Instead of cookies there were stacks of bookmarks with the new logo she'd worked out of Beans curled up with a book. It appeared also on the large sign outside announcing the hours of the Book Boutique.

The restroom was spotless and clearly marked, while

a "Staff Only" sign limited access to the kitchen and beyond. As far as she could see, all was ready.

She had driven herself mercilessly to make the opening happen on time. Please God, let it be worth our effort, she thought, remembering all the people, both professional and volunteers, whose names she'd put on a list to thank once this day was over.

Lynn, in her optimism, proved to be correct, as the rain slowed long enough for customers to begin drifting in about one-thirty. Nerissa left Gerard in the office and made herself available to answer questions and give tours. Lynn, Ross, and Keisha did the same.

"I've always wanted to read the book about black folk that DuBois wrote, and now that I'm retired I have the time," an elderly man told Nerissa.

"You mean *The Souls of Black Folk?*"

"That's the one. I know it's an old book," he said anxiously.

"I don't have it, but I can order it for you," she said.

"Good. I want my own copy so I can take as long as I like with it."

Nerissa was thrilled to put that down as the first order for the Book Boutique because it reflected her goal in providing books not easily accessible.

By three o'clock, the sun had come out, and there was a steady stream of people in and out. Some came just to look and promised to return. Some bought one or two books, especially from the fiction section, and a few bought several from both the fiction and the younger readers sections, as gifts, they said.

Hugh appeared with Lucy's family, and while they visited each room, he made a quick tour and spent the rest of the time looking at new books and talking to Nerissa when she wasn't busy.

"You're an awesome lady, getting this done in the short time since I met you," he said, lounging near the counter. "I can't imagine the hours you put in."

"I had a lot of help." She put a rubber band around two books and put them on the layaway shelf.

"I'd have been glad to help had I known." He emphasized glad. When she glanced at him, he added, "My evenings are usually open, Nerissa."

Since she was free for a moment, she asked curiously, "What do you do, Hugh?" She wondered if he modeled or was in entertainment. Somehow that was the impression she had of him.

"I'm with an accounting firm"—he shrugged his shoulders—"by day." A card bearing only his name and a telephone number appeared in front of her.

"Perhaps we could go out sometime." He leaned across the counter.

"I doubt that I'll have time to go out now that this store is open," she said, sliding the card back to him. If this were not a public place, she would have loved to tell him that it was not her policy to call a man for a date.

"Miss Nerissa, I love your bookstore," Josie said, placing one book on the counter. "Mama said that's the only book I can buy today, but I see some more I can get later."

She was followed by the rest of the family, and after they'd gone, Maggie Rose and Chris arrived.

"Did you see the baby books, Maggie Rose?" she asked. "I had you in mind when I ordered them."

"I haven't decided which one I want the most, but I will before I go. It's a lovely bookstore, Nerissa, you should do a lot of business. I want you to keep some fliers in the Mailroom. We businesswomen have to help each other out," she said.

"Don't leave out the HS Stables office, too," Chris said. "I was looking for Bill. Where is he?" He glanced at Nerissa.

"I've no idea," she said. "I haven't seen him today, but he sent these yesterday." She pointed to the bouquet.

"He probably got held up somewhere," Maggie Rose said.

Pearline and Harold were next, followed by Helen Reid and her sisters, who said the house made a good bookstore and that Millie couldn't come today as she had a cold.

Dan Denton came and visited with her, but said nothing about his absent brother, which she appreciated.

The stream of customers had become a trickle by four-thirty.

"Let's start closing up," she told her team. "Check each room to see it is in order."

"I'm ready to go," Lynn said, "but it was a good day. I had fun answering questions and showing people where different authors are. Wish I could work here every day like you, Gerard." Her voice was wistful.

"Hey. What about our play?" Keisha and Ross reminded her.

Keisha held out a camera. "I took some pictures, Miss Nerissa, when I had a chance. I don't know if they're any good, but you can have them for your scrapbook." Nerissa was so weary and so touched, she had to blink rapidly as she took the film, promising that everyone could have any copies they wanted.

When she and Lynn got home, the other driveway was empty. It didn't matter. Her throat was scratchy, and she was tired in every bone. All she wanted to do was take something for her throat and crawl in bed so she'd be ready for tomorrow at the Book Boutique.

But she couldn't help wondering where Bill Denton was. He knew this was her big day. The bouquet was nice, but today his presence would have been more meaningful.

He was just like Ric. She knew it was true, and that was why she had to discipline her tendency to respond to the attraction between them. Still, the disappointment was deeper each time something happened.

When she'd been appointed head librarian and her colleagues had gathered to honor her, Ric hadn't been there.

Bill hadn't been there today. His brother had come; so had his best friend. But he'd neither come nor called. He was undependable. Like Ric.

She turned in her bed trying to get comfortable.

Her Book Boutique hopefully would turn out to be successful, but her personal life was going to be lonely and she'd better get used to it.

Chapter 22

"Where are all the people you said would be here?" Bill looked at his watch for the third time in the last half hour.

"They're coming. It's the rain that's slowed them down," the man standing next to him said.

The professor who hosted Bill's workshops had hired his services for the first humanitarian awards dinner at a large church in Columbia. Since it was supposed to start at noon and end at two-thirty, Bill had accepted. He would still be able get to the opening of the Book Boutique.

Now it was already twelve-thirty, and people were just beginning to come into the large dining room. Finally the dinner was served, followed by a speech about the occasion, and then the awards were presented.

He took the last picture at three-fifteen and left the church almost running. With luck on his side he could still make it by five. But luck was against him. The rain had also caused a serious accident on the interstate, and all traffic was backed up for half an hour.

He took out his cell phone and called Nerissa's number. No answer. He'd hoped to leave her a message, but the answering machine wasn't on. Why did people have such machines if they didn't turn them on? He didn't have a number for the bookstore, but maybe he could get it from information.

At last something was working right. He dialed the number.

"Hello," a male voice answered.

"Is this the Book Boutique?" Maybe he had the wrong number after all.

"Yes, it is."

Thank God. "May I speak with Nerissa Ramsey?"

"If you wait a minute, I'll try to find her."

Surely she would understand when he explained why he wasn't there. He could hear noise over the phone of conversation and movement, but no Nerissa. Had the person forgotten to get her? Who was it that answered the phone in the first place? It sounded like a kid. Could it have been Ross?

He held the phone to his ear with increasing impatience. What was going on? He repressed a desire to yell into the phone out of a frustration to let someone on the other end know he was still there.

Then the connection was broken.

He took the phone from his ear and looked at it in disbelief. Someone had hung up on him. For a wild moment he wanted to throw the phone out the window into the rain and let the next car crush it.

Now what? Traffic wasn't moving. He looked at his watch. He was sunk. It was nearly five. He had nothing to lose, so he'd try again. The line was busy.

That was it. He put the cell away. He'd done the best he could. Thank God he'd had the flowers delivered yesterday. That should help his case.

He was tired and depressed by the time he got to Jamison, and he still had to go by his parents' house. Maybe he'd ride by Nerissa's first to see if she was home.

Her pickup was in the driveway, and a light was on. His knock was answered by Lynn.

"Is Nerissa home, Lynn?"

"She's in bed, Mr. Bill. She didn't feel good by the time we got home. Did you want me to tell her anything?" she asked curiously.

"Just that I stopped by."

"Okay. Good night, Mr. Bill."

There was nothing good about it. He'd made a mistake going to Columbia. But it was too late now.

The next day he kept an appointment with Evelyn Hightower, assistant principal at the high school.

"You know we like the work you've done for us in the past, Bill, and now we have another project we hope you'll take on."

"If I can do it, I'll be glad to help," Bill said and in the next moment wondered if their project would interfere with his Nova Scotia venture.

"We've obtained funding for a pilot program with the creative arts and we want to include photography. We thought that might interest students who pass up music, drama, and painting. It would only last six weeks and be restricted to a certain number of students who show real enthusiasm for it. How does that sound to you?" Her beige suit and gold jewelry complemented her coffee-colored skin and her dark eyes smiled at Bill as she leaned toward him. "Do you think it's worth doing?"

"Absolutely. I do workshops for college students, and I'd love to start with kids at this level. My only problem would be time." He told her about the Nova Scotia trip.

"That's great, Bill. You have no idea yet when you'll be gone?"

"No, but I expect to hear from them by the end of this month. When is your pilot program starting?"

"Not until mid-January. You'll let me know as soon as you hear, won't you? Then we can see how to work it out."

Six weeks with a lot of high school kids. Now that could be fun getting them to learn the basics and sending them out on assignments. There was so much to see in this area, so much they could learn about seeing with the inner eye as well as with the camera lens.

This appointment had turned out really well. His next one might not, but good or bad, he intended to clear up certain matters with Nerissa Ramsey.

When he drove up to the Book Boutique, he saw that the only other vehicle there was her pickup. Good. No one to interrupt them.

She was in her office and so was her blasted cat. Both pairs of green eyes looked at him across the counter.

"Hello, Nerissa," he said, pinning her with a glance.

"Hello, Bill." No smile. She was logging in some books at the computer. *So that's the way she wants to play it,* he thought.

"How did it go yesterday?" he asked.

"Very well, and thanks for the flowers." She picked up a book and glanced at the title.

She could try to ignore him, but he knew how to get under her skin.

"I'm glad it went well. Anyone there that I might know?" he asked pleasantly as he relaxed against the counter.

"Only about half of the people who bothered to attend,"

she began. He saw the agitation rise in her as she stood up, straightened her shoulders in that familiar gesture, and tilted her chin as she came to stand opposite him.

"The Peebles family came, including Hugh, who spent most of his time with me. Then there were Chris and Maggie Rose. And your brother Dan. And Jim Phillips and Ross's family. And Pearline and Harold. And Jerlene and Matt and Covey. They were all here."

He saw the question in her eyes, and he could have answered it. That was too easy. He wanted to make her forget her pride and ask where he was. Then he'd know it meant something to her. So he waited, holding her gaze.

"You were otherwise engaged, I take it," she said coolly.

If he hadn't been so wary of walking on eggshells with her, he'd have laughed out loud. She'd managed to ask what she wanted to know without sacrificing her pride. He loved her smart wit.

"I'll be happy to tell you where I was," he said. "I was working at a church in Columbia at an awards dinner. It was supposed to start at noon and be over at two-thirty, which would have put me here about four. But they were very late starting. Then the rain slowed the traffic down. Then there was a serious accident that tied up the interstate for half an hour."

He saw her expression soften a fraction, so he continued. "I called your house from the car, but your answering machine wasn't on. I didn't know the number here but got it through Directory Assistance. Then do you know what happened, Nerissa?"

He could feel his frustration rising as it had yesterday.

"No, I don't know," she said, picking up a pen.

"I called. A male voice answered, and when I asked for you, he told me to wait and he'd get you. I waited, and waited, and waited, Nerissa. Then someone hung up on me."

Now he saw a flicker in her eyes and a frown on her face.

"No one's supposed to answer the phone except me and Gerard, my new clerical assistant. But he never told me about a phone call," she said, and made a note on a pad.

"I called back and the line was busy, so I gave up as it was nearly five." Could she see how he'd tried to make it? It wasn't his fault that the people were late, that it rained, that there'd been an accident. It was an unfortunate chain of events, and at the end he hadn't been at her opening.

There was a knock at the front door. He saw it was a delivery man with a big box.

"I'll get it," he said, and held the door while the man came in and set it on the floor in the office, waited for Nerissa to sign for it, and left.

Bill spoke quickly before he lost her attention as he saw her eyeing the box.

"Nerissa, I wanted to be here with you yesterday, and I'm really sorry it didn't work out." He reached across the counter to touch her fingertips.

"I can see you tried." Her eyes warmed, and a little smile quirked her lips.

The temperature in the room soared. "I went by your house when I got into town. Lynn said you were in bed. You feeling better now?" he asked anxiously. The lady didn't know how to take care of herself, always working too hard. It worried him.

She looked surprised. "I didn't know you came by. Lynn must have forgotten to tell me before she rushed off this morning." Another note on her pad.

"You're not doing too great in getting your messages," he said. "Want me to train your helpers? I'll do it for free." He wanted to see her smile again.

She came around the counter to look at the wooden crate as she smiled at him. "I'll train my helpers, but you can open this for me if you don't mind."

"What's in it?" he asked as he worked the nails loose.

"Some African items I'd hoped would get here for yesterday. I want to put them around for decoration and to heighten interest in our heritage."

There were two masks, several baskets, a number of bowls, and some lengths of cloth.

"Do you like them?" She held up each article for his inspection.

"Very much. Looking at them reminds me, Nerissa, are you insured?" She might not think it was his business, but she needed to be insured.

"Of course," she said as she put the pieces behind the counter.

"What time does your assistant come?" he wanted to know.

"As soon as he gets out of class, and that varies, but he's never later than three. Why do you ask?" She looked at the cat as she scratched its back.

"That means you're in here alone from the time you open." He looked over into the next room and then down the hall. "There's a lot of space here."

"This is a business, you know, and I'll have customers in and out," she said defensively.

"Sure, but not all the time, which means you'll be vulnerable if a guy wants to come in and rob you." Couldn't she see the danger she might be in?

"I can take care of myself. You don't need to worry." She took the cat up in her arms and stroked it as she looked at him calmly.

"Why are you being so stubborn?" All he was trying to do was make her see some sense.

Her chin came up. "I'm stubborn because I don't agree with you." The cat meowed as she tightened her arms around him. "Sorry, Beans," she said and let him go.

The cat leapt from the counter, and the next thing Bill knew it was wrapping itself around his leg. "Get away from me, cat," he said, and shook his leg.

Between the cat and Nerissa, he was frustrated all over again.

"No, you're stubborn because you were born that way. Can't you see that I worry about you? Or are you too stubborn to see that as well?"

He saw her eyes widen as if a new idea had occurred to her, and he felt a flutter somewhere inside. He couldn't look away.

The door opened, and a group of people came in. Nerissa blinked, then came around the counter to greet them.

"We couldn't get here yesterday," he heard a woman say.

"See you later," he told Nerissa.

"Thanks for stopping by," she replied, ushering the group into the fiction room.

A young guy with a book bag passed him on the porch. That was probably her assistant. It eased his mind to know she wouldn't be alone in the building.

It was ironic that they lived next door, yet *alone* was how he could never get her, he thought, backing out into the street.

She wouldn't go to dinner with him and even if he went to her house, they wouldn't be alone. Either Lynn or that cat would interrupt.

He still had questions to ask, and number one on the list had to do with her ex-husband.

Was it his resemblance to her ex that made her back away every time they made the slightest move toward friendship?

Chapter 23

Nerissa looked at the local paper with pride. BOOK BOUTIQUE A WELCOME ADDITION, the caption read. Below it was a picture showing her in the history room with the African masks on the wall. The article mentioned that the store specialized in books by and about black people and provided an often neglected resource. It quoted her as promising, "If we don't have it, we'll order it."

This was the result of her stopping by the paper last week with an invitation to the opening. The reporter had visited two days later, and now here was this free publicity. She made a note to tell them thanks and to get copies to send to Seattle.

Tomorrow she'd laminate the story and post it.

"Ready to go, Gerard?" she called.

"Yes, ma'am." He came in from the back rooms with two misplaced books. "A lady asked me today if we were going to carry black greeting cards, Miss Nerissa. I said I'd ask." Gerard looked like he could be playing basketball, and he was an honor student already taking pre-college courses.

"You may tell her it's the next thing we're planning," Nerissa said. When she'd questioned him about the phone call from Bill, he said he hadn't taken it, but in the confusion of new people coming in, there were times when neither of them had been in the office. One of them must always be in the office from now on, she'd decided.

She checked all the locks and left. The place was still so new to her that she frequently just stood and looked at it. Her dream come true. Even Miss Millie had looked into every nook and cranny and said she knew her mama would appreciate the care Nerissa had given it.

At home she got dinner on the table quickly. This was the night of the Christmas play.

"Mom and Dad called to wish me luck. And Grace. I'm so excited. It would be perfect if they were here. " Lynn dabbed at her mouth with her napkin.

"Maybe you can send them some pictures," Nerissa suggested.

"Keisha always has her camera. Could you use it and get pictures of us in our costumes?" Lynn asked.

"Don't know how good they'll be, but I'll take them," she said, and resolutely put her mind on other topics while repressing the image of the man next door who usually had a camera around his neck or in his hands. Those hands that could be so caressing and so comforting.

She caught herself still at the sink with plates to be put in the dishwasher and scolded herself about wishful thinking.

Lynn and Ross piled in the pickup just as Bill was getting out of his car.

"Hi, Mr. Bill," Lynn called. "You coming to the play tonight?"

He came over and stood at Nerissa's window. "Hey," he said to her softly. "Wish I could see you kids, but I have to work." Then to Nerissa, "You all right?"

"I'm fine. How about you?" How could his simple greeting manage to sound so personal and caring?

"Okay. Have a great time and be careful, all of you." He stepped away.

She went out of the driveway, and as she turned into the street she glanced through the rearview mirror. He was still watching.

The auditorium was full and the play went off well. Lynn's portrayal of The Ghost of Christmas Past brought down the house. Backstage afterward, Nerissa asked Lucy, "Were you satisfied with the production?"

"Yes. I told the kids I wanted this to be the best play, and they made it so. One more day of school, and then two blessed weeks off. Let's try to get together one evening."

Nerissa and Lynn shopped for gifts and mailed a number of them to Seattle. They bought a tree, and Ross and Keisha helped them decorate it.

On Christmas Eve, Lynn said, 'We're going caroling, Aunt Rissa. Want to come with us?"

It was a lovely night, and for a moment she was tempted. "I don't think so. I'll have some hot chocolate ready when you come back."

She couldn't help but be grateful for Lynn being there. It made a real difference, especially when it came to the holidays. It kept her from being alone.

She put on a CD of traditional carols and settled back to finish wrapping some gifts, stopping every once in a while to enjoy the sparkling tree.

There was a quiet knock at the door. Bill stood there with a Santa Claus hat tipped forward on his head and a sheepish smile on his face.

"Merry Christmas," he said.

"Come in, Santa." She couldn't help but laugh, he looked so funny. "Have a seat."

"I've been doing some Christmas baking, and when I saw you were home, I thought I'd bring yours right away." He handed her a foil-wrapped round loaf.

She unwrapped it. "I love this kind of bread with nuts and fruit. You've even braided it! Let's have some right away. I'll put on some fresh coffee while you tell me how you made it."

When the coffee was ready, she had him cut the bread, and she put everything on tray tables so they could sit in the living room.

She saw Beans come into the room and immediately rub against Bill's leg. She waited for his usual growl, but he only moved his leg away. She smiled over the rim of her cup, wondering if he'd learned that Beans would leave him alone after that one rub.

She buttered a piece of the bread and popped it in her mouth. Bill was watching her as she chewed the flavorful morsel. "Delicious."

His eyes gleamed with pleasure. "I'm really glad you like it," he said, sampling it now.

"How did you start baking?" She was eager to learn anything about him that she could, to get below the surface and discover more of the man himself.

"I've always liked to eat, so I messed around in the kitchen and pestered my mom until she saw I was serious. Then she didn't bother me when I said I wanted to make something. When I went away to school, I cooked for myself and made extra money cooking for some of the guys in the dorm."

"Did you ever think of becoming a chef?" Beans meowed at her side, and she gave him a few crumbs from her plate.

"Only in my own kitchen. I always knew I wanted to make my living with photography. Cooking is simply an enjoyable hobby. But it's also a stress reliever." He winked at her and she could see the same boyish aspect that had inspired him to wear the Santa cap. "Some days nothing goes right, and instead of kicking the side of the car, I create a new dish or bake bread. I can pummel the dough instead of a person."

"I know exactly what you mean," she said. "Gardening gives me my outlet when I'm frustrated. The earth is something I can always count on. It never changes, and it rewards my efforts if I work at it." She turned her gaze from the tree to look at Bill. Would he understand how she felt? Ric never had.

"I think it's even more than that for you as far as I can see," he said, his gaze intent on her. "It's a way you express beauty. Anyone can see that when they look at what you've done here, especially with the azaleas."

His simple statement showed a discernment that surprised and pleased her. Had she been underestimating him all these weeks? She busied herself refilling his cup and changed the subject.

"I know you do studio sittings like the one I saw of Breia and Josie, and you told me about Mrs. Martin's request. That's all I know about your work. What else has it covered since college?"

She saw that he recognized the sincerity of her interest, and she became completely absorbed as he described work he'd done for magazines, newspapers, books, and institutions. Her questions generated anecdotes related to some of his work. He told them with a simplicity and humor that was entertaining. Nevertheless, she was beginning to grasp the depth and notability of what he had accomplished in his profession. It was no wonder Nova Scotia had selected him for their project.

"Why haven't you," she began, "or should I say, have you considered publishing a book of your photography?" It sounded logical to her.

He seemed pleased by her implication that he could do such a thing. He touched her hand and smiled. "Are you flattering me?" he asked.

"Not at all. You surely have the ability. Do you mean you've never thought of it?" That was hard to believe.

He laughed. "Sure, when I was a brash young fellow just out of college. However, as I understood more about the complexities of photography, I brushed that thought away and concentrated on learning. I guess that's one of the reasons this Nova Scotia trip is so fascinating. It'll be the nearest I'll come to producing a book of my work on a given subject."

As the hours passed, their conversation changed, so that although photography and gardening were their topics, she felt that on a subterranean level, they were increasing their knowledge of each other.

With knowledge was supposed to come understanding, the adage went. She pushed her empty plate away and looked at him speculatively. Did he understand that it rankled her every month when she paid her rent, knowing her ability as a responsible tenant was being questioned? She'd proven herself over and over, so why didn't he tear up that offending lease and give her a new one? It might be a small matter to someone else, but not to her.

He finished his bread and reached for his napkin, then looked at her. "What is it, Nerissa?" he asked, a little frown appearing on his forehead. He must have seen the query in her eyes.

Before she could answer, the door opened and Lynn, Ross, and Keisha came in.

Her question would have to wait for another time. She sensed that he'd had one for her as well.

The problem was that she wasn't sure whether the answers to their questions would be what either of them wanted to hear.

Chapter 24

"Bill, I've misplaced my list," his mother said on the phone. "Must be something wrong with my brain. I get more forgetful every day." She laughed self-deprecatingly. "How many loaves of white and how many of wheat did you say you'd make?"

"Five of each, Mom. Do you need more?" he asked, looking at the loaves sitting on their racks.

"No, that's fine. You'll bring them today?"

"Sometime in the early afternoon. That soon enough?"

"The committee is coming at noon to make up the bags. The people will be so thankful to have good, home-made bread. We sure appreciate your helping us, son."

"I like doing it. Are you going to get some rest? You run yourself ragged every year during the holidays." He knew it did no good to tell her to rest, but he had to do it anyway. She never seemed to stop working for her various charities.

"You and your dad are just alike. He wouldn't let me get up my usual time this morning because I had a lit-tle headache." She gave that hearty chuckle he liked to hear. "See you later, Bill," she said.

He put the phone down and got out a large mixing bowl. He guessed he didn't need to worry about his mother's health as she was rarely ill. It was more of a habit than anything else. He put several bars of chocolate to melt in the microwave and proceeded to mix up enough brownies to fill two large baking pans. Tomorrow he would take the brownies and perhaps some coffee cake to the Jenkins Orphanage and The Shelter, his own private charities.

Business was slow for him after Christmas. Often he used the time for a holiday trip of some sort, but not this year. He was content to stay home anticipating word from Nova Scotia, organizing his files, basking in the glow of his unexpected evening with Nerissa, and being inspired to make a special dessert for each of his siblings. Now that he knew Nerissa liked bread with fruit and nuts, he decided to make her his richest fruitcake. He couldn't give it to her right away, but he could get it made and put it away to ripen.

Dan showed up one afternoon with their parents in tow. "I came to pick up my chocolate Kahlua cake and brought mom and dad along for the ride," he explained.

"I want to look at that house you bought," his dad said.

"I can't take you inside, of course," Bill told him as they all tramped outside, "but you can see what Nerissa's done to the outside of the house and to the yard."

After examining both front and back, his mom said decisively, "I'd say you were lucky to get her. No man could have done better."

Dan sent him a knowing glance over their mother's head.

"She did all this work herself?" his dad asked.

"Harold fixed the shutters and Ross helped clean the

yard, but the rest of it is her labor." He tried not to sound too proud or possessive.

"What does this remarkable young lady do?" his mom asked.

"She opened a bookstore a week or so ago. Dan, why don't you take them by there so they can meet her? I'll follow you."

"Be glad to." Dan was so smug, Bill wondered if that had been his brother's intent all along.

Bill saw a few people in the other rooms at the Book Boutique, but Nerissa was alone in the office, which gave his parents an opportunity to visit with her after the introductions.

"You wouldn't happen to have a book about Harlem, would you?" his dad asked.

"About the entertainment aspect of it or the history?" Nerissa asked.

"I'm more interested in the history."

"I have a book by Jervis Anderson called *This Was Harlem*. It's in the history section. Bill, would you show him where that is, please?" She gave him a smile.

They found the book, and as he leafed through it, his dad said, "This is the one I want. Wait 'til Ed tries to give me some info now. I got the facts to prove I'm right."

His dad's constant arguments with his old friend Ed were well-known to all the family, and Nerissa, as the person who was going to make it possible for him to crow over Ed, automatically had a place in his esteem.

"I'll be back with some ladies from my church, Nerissa," he heard his mom say. "Then I can take my time and see what I want. I like your bookstore."

"Thank you for coming." To Bill she said, "Thanks for bringing them."

"Very interesting young woman. Not at all your usual type, Bill," his mother observed when they were outside. Dan chuckled at the surprised look on Bill's face, while his dad said, "She's an astute person. I can't wait to read this book."

All he could think on the way home was, how did mothers do that?

The next day, he ran into Nerissa and Lynn in the drugstore.

"Any word yet from Nova Scotia?" Nerissa asked. It was cold outside and she was bundled up in a red scarf with only her nose and eyes showing.

"Nothing yet. You look like Rudolph." He grinned. "It's not that cold here."

"It is to me." Lynn had wandered off to another aisle while Nerissa stood by the book display. She picked up a Nora Roberts book and glanced at the back cover.

"You read romance novels, Nerissa?" Somehow he'd thought the reading choice of a librarian would be different.

"I read a little bit of everything." She looked at him curiously. "Why not romance?"

"No reason. I guess I think of them as shallow." He shrugged.

"That's where you're wrong. They explore relationships between men and women in an honest way, especially in matters of trust. The characters work through their problems and always come to a happy ending. That's neither shallow nor easy." He saw the challenge in her green eyes, daring him to argue her point.

He was walking on eggshells again. He sensed that how he responded was important to her. "You're right, Nerissa. Caring for someone is one thing, but getting two people to trust one another is hard even when you try."

He heard himself say the words, saw how her eyes lightened, and realized the truth of what he'd said. No matter how attracted to each other they were, could they honestly say that trust was a part of the equation?

He didn't think so. There was attraction, chemistry, whatever you wanted to call it, perhaps some respect on both sides, but not trust.

At odd moments throughout the day, he tried to define to himself what he meant. He was handicapped by his resemblance to her ex, so that was a built-in factor for mistrust on her part. Not telling her about his connection to DB deepened it, and although she accepted his apology later, he wondered if it had erased the damage. He wasn't at the opening, which from her point of view might be another reason not to trust him. He couldn't say for sure; how women analyzed men's actions was often a mystery to him.

But how about him trusting her? She'd never lied or been dishonest, so far as he knew. So why didn't he feel he could trust her? Maybe it was because she'd never confided in him about her marriage, what the problems had been, and how it had affected her. The details you could tell to someone you trusted, knowing they wouldn't judge you, and that the telling would bring you closer together because you'd shared that painful part of your life.

The more he thought about it, the more he saw he'd touched a hurtful place in himself.

The other reason was that every time they made a little progress toward each other, she'd take a step back or sideways the next time they had any contact. In other words, he couldn't depend on her emotions.

He found himself at the window, looking at her house and asking himself, is it worth it? He'd be thirty-five soon, and he'd never gone through such emotional turmoil about a woman.

The answer rose up in his consciousness, clear as a bell. He had no choice. This relationship was, in her words, neither shallow nor easy. No matter what the outcome, he had to see it through.

As the last days of the month slid by, and he heard nothing from Nova Scotia, he became more and more anxious. If this was how Nerissa had felt as she searched for a building, he could sympathize with her. Every day he listened to his messages carefully and read his e-mail. Finally, when he could stand the suspense no longer, he called the number Maren Johnson had given him. The voice asked him to please leave a message. He did and waited for a return call that never came. It must be that people were away for the holiday season. But she had said by December thirtieth.

He asked Nerissa to go out with him New Year's Eve, but she'd promised to chaperone a party for Lynn and her friends at the house.

On New Year's Day he slept late, then hung out with Dan and later with Chris and Maggie Rose. He ended up at his parents' for a late snack and went home feeling more down than up.

He was grateful to have three jobs during the next two days and spent the rest of the time worrying about Nova Scotia and gathering his accounts to send to his tax accountant.

The following day he received a letter with a Canadian stamp. At last! He hurried in the house, slit it open, and a single-page letter came out. He read it eagerly, then once more disbelievingly.

> *Dear Mr. Denton: We are devastated to have to tell you that the Nova Scotia project has lost its funding. We hasten to send this news to you at once and will return your entry packet and refund your entry fee as soon as possible. We have done everything we could to prevent this from happening, but to no avail. Please accept our apologies, and we hope that in the future you will visit Nova Scotia and make your own photographic pilgrimage.*
>
> *Sincerely yours,*
> *Maren Johnson*

Chapter 25

"There has to be a mistake," Bill raged. "This just can't be right! Where is that phone number?"

He strode into his office, grabbed the Nova Scotia file out of the cabinet, located and dialed the number for Maren Johnson. He was going to speak to her or someone and get to the bottom of this.

The ringing stopped. He started to speak, then realized that the voice he heard was saying, "The number you have reached is no longer in service."

Maybe he could find another name or phone number. He searched through the magazine article, but there was only the address to which he'd sent his application.

The article gave as the source of the funding matching money from agencies and private donors to be combined with a grant from the Arts Council.

That's where the problem was. He knew it to be a frequent issue with anything connected with the humanities and the arts. They weren't valued as highly as athletics, for instance, or politically feasible projects.

Knowing that didn't keep him from being angry. He'd been deeply invested in this whole idea, not only because of his emotional connection with the Underground Railroad taking slaves to freedom, but also because it had given him an entirely new direction for his work. A stimulus he'd needed even more than he'd realized.

This year, through the Nova Scotia undertaking, he'd anticipated exploring fresh ideas and themes through his camera. He'd felt it would turn out to be the means of launching him upon new and higher levels in his work.

Now it was all down the drain.

When Chris called that night to say the Christmas ad and Bill's photo had been successful in getting new students, and then asked when he was going to Nova Scotia, Bill told him the news.

"Man, that's rough. I know you'd been looking forward to it. No chance of it happening later?" Chris asked.

"Not that I can see."

"Come to dinner tomorrow?"

"Later, Chris, but thanks." He wasn't ready for an evening with Chris and Maggie Rose yet.

In the next few days, he talked only with people he had to talk with. He avoided everyone else. He was under a black cloud he found hard to lift and spent most of his time when he wasn't with a client roaming around the area with his camera, photographing winter scenes: leafless trees standing next to some with green leaves; a dry lawn with shriveled borders contrasted with healthy redtip shrubs and beds of pansies; a cabin in the middle of a deserted field; the remains of a two-story house, porch fallen in, windows gone, vines growing up the sides and almost encircling it; through a few barren trees, a shack with a rocking chair on the porch and smoke coming from the chimney. It was visible to him now only because the leaves that concealed it the rest of the year were gone.

These images, part of the Low Country he loved, seemed to reduce some of his agitation. They spoke to a subconscious part of his identity, and he began to feel a little better. More like who he was, and that made him suddenly long to talk to Nerissa about the situation.

He waited until after dinner one night to call.

"Nerissa. This is Bill. Are you busy?"

"Not especially. Why?"

"I need to see you. May I come over?"

"Of course."

She opened the door, seated him on the couch beside her and, looking at him intently, asked "What happened?"

"I'm not going to Nova Scotia." He found those were the only words he could get out at that moment.

"I don't understand. You mean they changed their mind about you?" Her voice rose.

"No. They lost their funding, and it all fell through," he said dully.

"Oh, Bill." The acute sympathy in her voice reached him, and he turned to meet her steady, warm gaze. "It meant so much to you. I can't tell you how very sorry I am that you aren't going."

He felt that if he kept looking, he could drown in the softness of her tender response. It drew him like a magnet. This was what he needed, to be close to her, to feel her heart beating next to his. He reached out for her, and she came willingly into his arms.

He knew that losing the project wasn't his fault, yet he'd felt as if he'd been found wanting. It had been an embarrassment. He'd only told Chris, not even his parents or Dan, because he felt somehow diminished.

Now, holding Nerissa in a close embrace, reassurance

began to flow through him. Her nearness was a salve to his wounded self-esteem.

He gave her a long, lingering kiss. When he lifted his head to look at her, she was flushed, her eyes bright. She put her arms around his neck, and the sweetness of her kiss went through his veins in a buoyant flood.

"You'll get through this," she whispered.

He nodded and kissed her again.

"My sweet Nerissa," he said. Each kiss left him yearning for more.

"There's a connection between us," he said, certain of this truth. He held her face between his hands, searching her eyes.

She put her hands on his. "I know," she said, her eyes glowing.

He heard a door open, and he moved away from Nerissa just as the cat came in, followed by Lynn.

"Hi, Mr. Bill. I didn't know you were here," Lynn said, holding an open book in her hand. "I didn't mean to interrupt you, Aunt Rissa."

"You need some help?" Nerissa asked.

"It can wait," she said, scooping up the cat and leaving the room.

"I'd totally forgotten she was here," Bill said as he rose from the couch. "Can I persuade you to come over to my house one evening?" He took her hands in his, raised her from the couch, and pulled her into his arms. He felt he could take a chance on Lynn not coming right back in, as he kissed Nerissa again. "Will you come?" he asked.

"Yes," she promised. "Call me."

***

Anyone opening a business had to anticipate problems, and Nerissa was no exception. However, the one she faced in early January was unexpected at this point in her plans.

Gerard had said, "Miss Nerissa, I have to talk to you," anxiety in his expression.

They were closing up the store, and he was fiddling with the strap of his book bag before putting it over his shoulders.

"Sure, Gerard. What is it?" Since this was a departure from his usual conversation, Nerissa stood still to listen.

"I hate to say it, but I can't work here anymore." The words came in a rush, as if he were reluctant to say them. Then he seemed relieved that the worst was over.

Nerissa was surprised and upset. Had something gone wrong that she didn't know about?

"Why not, Gerard? Are you having problems here?"

"No, it's nothing like that," he said quickly.

She felt better knowing that whatever it was, the store was okay.

"It's my school work. This is my last semester, and I thought I could put in the hours here and still do all I have to do to keep up my grades, but I can't do it. Getting ready for college has to be the first thing for me, even though I do want to earn some money, too." His sudden smile highlighted his boyishness, and she thought it was easy to forget how young he was because of the excellence of his conduct in the store.

"I hate to let you go, Gerard, but I do understand. Is this your last day?" She hoped not, since the coming weekend was always busy.

"I'll be here tomorrow and Saturday—if that's okay?"

"That's fine, and I'll give you your check on Saturday."

What a setback, she thought, during the evening. The Book Boutique hadn't been open a full month yet, and already she had to deal with staffing needs.

Relying on part-time employees was always a risk, but that was what she had budgeted for this first year. Now she had to rethink that part of her program. Should she stay with the plan and find another part-timer or figure out how she could pay a full-time person?

That was certainly preferable. A person like Helen Reid of the Craft Corner, who was retired but wanted to earn a supplemental income. Or a retired teacher who wasn't ready to stay home yet.

The next day she talked to Helen Reid, Lucy Davis, and Maggie Rose about the situation. Three of the people they suggested were female. The fourth, a man retired from the military, was divorced, trim, and scholarly. Even if he turned out to never be anything but friendly, she felt there were too many other risks in hiring him, including how the mostly female customers would respond to him.

One of the three women lived with her daughter, who had a small child, and she admitted that sometimes she might be called upon to watch the child.

The other two, Nellie Weber and Sarah Clawson, were both pleasant and qualified, especially Ms. Weber, who was a retired schoolteacher.

Sarah Clawson had worked at various clerical jobs but stopped working to nurse her husband through his final illness sixteen months ago.

"I'm through the worst of that now, and I'm ready to be out with people every day," she said cheerfully.

A lifelong reader, she was thrilled at the possibility of working with books.

"If I had this job, I'd probably spend most of my salary buying books," she told Nerissa. "You've got a lot of great titles."

"You'd get an employee discount, which would help a little," Nerissa told her. "When could you begin?"

"Now, if you want me. There's only me and my cat," she said, all smiles.

They agreed that she would begin the next day, and that she would work a thirty-four-hour week at minimum wage to start. "We'll look at this again in six months," Nerissa said.

At home that evening, Nerissa called Lucy to thank her.

"When you leave the high school, you can start an employment agency," she said teasingly.

"I'll keep that in mind," Lucy chuckled.

The phone rang again as soon as Lucy hung up.

"Hi. It's me," Bill said. "Can you come over? I just took a pie out of the oven."

"Are you tempting me?" she asked, a smile in her voice.

"I sure hope so."

"See you in a few minutes."

Chapter 26

The wind had been blowing all day, and even though Nerissa was going just across the yard, she put on a heavy sweater. As she came out onto her porch, she saw that the wind had strengthened.

She wrapped her arms around herself and bowed her head in an effort to keep her balance against the force of the wind. It pushed her along and almost propelled her up his steps.

The door opened before she could knock.

"It's cold out there," Bill said. "I know just how to warm you up." He smiled and took her in his arms.

They were almost the same height, she thought, which made them fit together as they held each other.

"Warm?" he murmured against her hair.

"Mmmm," she said, feeling cozy and secure.

He set his palms against her face. "I've been wanting to kiss you here, and here, and especially here," he said as he nipped at her ear, her bottom lip, and a spot on her neck so sensitive it made her shiver.

It also made her aware that they were still standing just inside the door, and already her nerves were dancing.

She took a small step back. "Good evening to you,

too," she said. 'Someone promised me pie fresh from the oven. What kind is it?"

"Apple walnut." He took her hand and led her to the kitchen, where the fragrance of his baking filled the air.

"Smells great." She sat at the table and loosened her sweater.

He brought pie and coffee to the table, then sat across from her. "What's new at the store?" he asked as he began cutting the pie.

"Gerard quit so he could put more time in on his lessons this last semester, he said." She gave him the details, glad to have an impersonal subject to talk about.

"You're not going to be there alone, are you?" He held her plate in his hand, a small frown puckering his forehead.

"No. I hired a new person today, a woman named Sarah Clawson. She'll be working full-time, five days a week." She described Sarah and why she chose her instead of the other applicants while he filled her cup and placed the pie in front of her.

"The thing I like about her is that she has a personal interest in the books we sell."

She stopped to taste the pie. The flaky crust, the spicy apples, and the walnuts with a hint of caramel made a delicious combination.

"You seriously missed your calling, Bill." She closed her eyes a second. "I have to savor this, slowly." She licked her lips and noticed the pie on his plate was untouched.

"Why aren't you eating?" she asked, her fork midway in the air.

He smiled crookedly. "I'm too busy watching you.

Eating I can do anytime, but I can't always have you at my table." He raised his cup. "To you."

She touched her cup to his. "To you."

Sitting across from him was like trying to keep her balance while the force of what he'd called the connection between them filled the air. She asked about his parents and had he seen Maggie Rose and Chris. What other mundane subject could she bring up?

"Have you always had your studio here in your house?" She ate the last of her pie.

"No, when I left the university I rented a very small space on Main Street." He pushed his empty plate aside. "It was near the jewelry store but now it's incorporated into the insurance building. When I began making an income I could count on, I bought this house and built my own studio. Let me show it to you."

One whole side of the house was his studio. It held a small office and gallery, a larger room that Breia and Josie had described, where sittings were held, a section for his files and work space, and a darkroom at the end.

His hand touched her as he steered her around a chair and again to keep her from stumbling over a pile of books. He stood close while he talked about some of his pictures lining the wall.

She was acutely aware of his touch and his nearness; the air seemed to quiver between them. She had to leave just as soon as this studio tour was over.

She focused her attention on a black and white picture of a house taken from a side view. The windows were broken, the roof of the porch slanted diagonally at one edge, and tall weeds partially obscured the front of the building, yet she couldn't stop looking at it. She felt the presence of people, and wasn't that a face peering out of one of the two front windows?

"Where did you see this house?" she finally asked.

"In a field out in the country. There're a lot of deserted houses, sheds, and barns around, and some of them have a story to tell if you take your time with the camera. You like that one?" She heard something in his voice that was more than curiosity.

Instead of answering his question, she said, "I keep thinking I see a face in that front window."

"You see it?" he said excitedly.

She turned to him questioningly. "I don't understand."

"Of all the people who've been through here, you're the only one who's spoken of the face." His eyes lit with intensity and locked onto hers.

"It's that connection between us," he said, catching her in a tight embrace. He bent his head and kissed her, hot and hard.

She felt herself begin to melt into him and with great effort pulled away from the whirlwind of emotion he effortlessly stirred in her.

She was desperately afraid of what he made her feel. When he'd come to her in need after the Nova Scotia letter, she'd had no choice but to follow her heart and give him comfort and warmth. But she shouldn't have come here tonight because she was being drawn into an enchantment that was increasingly hard to resist.

Like all enchantment, she knew it couldn't last.

Ric had met her when she was young, attractive, hopeful about the future, and trusting. She'd fallen in love with him with her whole innocent heart, believing in her marriage vows. To her, children were a part of marriage, and she yearned for the day when her body carried a child, the fruit of the love she and Ric shared.

Gradually she understood this was not what Ric wanted. He found excuses not to make love, and she suffered the misery of his rejection. It was when she saw the young woman pregnant with Ric's child that she gave up hope. For one terrible moment, her control had slipped and she wanted to cry out, "That's *my* baby you're carrying!"

She lost confidence in her desirability as a woman. Only her intellect and her pride were left.

She'd not felt the slightest attraction for any man until she met Bill. Was it because he resembled Ric, or was it the man himself?

Whatever it was, she couldn't trust it, so she put her hands on his chest to put distance between them.

"Nerissa?" His voice was husky, his breath warm, and his eyes filled with heat.

She searched frantically for something to say. "I came over because I wanted to talk to you, Bill."

He stared blankly at her. "About what?"

"About you."

"I'm talking about me now and how I feel." He tried to embrace her again.

"You're talking about us." She took a couple of steps away and gestured at the pictures they'd just seen. "I'm talking about you and this." She stood next to the desk and looked at him entreatingly.

He leaned against a counter. "What about this? I don't know what you're saying."

"What do you plan to do in place of going to Nova Scotia?" She watched him closely.

"I don't know, haven't gotten that far," he said in a clipped tone.

"It occurred to me yesterday that since you've been so focused on it, why let all that research and that energy go to waste? Go anyway. On your own." To her that was so sensible, and it excited her. He was too talented to let go what had occupied him for months and then had disappeared, leaving a big gaping hole. She knew that feeling, and she hoped she could persuade him to do something about it. Soon.

He looked at her unseeingly, and she knew he was analyzing her suggestion.

"That might work," he said thoughtfully. She saw the idea take hold, lighting a gleam in his eye.

"Would you go with me and do the writing? We could be collaborators." Now he smiled outright.

He surprised her. "I can't go, but that doesn't stop you."

"You're brilliant, Nerissa. The more I think of it, the better I like it." Enthusiasm rang in his voice.

"I can't go, Bill," she repeated. He obviously hadn't listened the first time she said it.

This time he heard. "But I need you to make it work, Nerissa. I can take the pictures, but I can't always put into words what it means. It's the camera that speaks for me. Don't you see?" He appealed for her to understand.

"I wasn't going with you the first time," she pointed out.

"I know, and I'd have muddled through somehow, but this time we'd be working side by side, seeing the places, talking to the people and sharing our thoughts. I can just see us." He was absolutely still, looking at her.

For a long moment she was caught up in his vision,

the two of them, partners, actually at the end of the Underground Railroad. Together. Creating something new.

He came to her and took her hands. "Wouldn't you like to do that, Nerissa?"

She couldn't deny it. "Of course I would. It'd be a great adventure."

"Then why can't you go with me?"

"I have a bookstore to run." Had he forgotten?

"I have a business to run, too, but we wouldn't have to be away too long."

How many ways did she have to say it? She was ready to weep at having to keep saying no when every fiber in her being wanted to say yes.

"Take someone else. I can't go."

They stood toe to toe. She felt him exerting the full strength of his personality to persuade her to say she'd go with him. It was a kind of strength she'd never seen in a man she had to deal with.

But her will was strong too. She thought that was a part of their mutual attraction. An element of excitement was always present when they were together.

"I opened the bookstore only a few weeks ago, and I can't go running off into the wild blue yonder just because I feel like it. Can't you see that, Bill?" *Please understand.*

"Suppose I wanted you to do a Low Country book with me. Would you do it?"

She didn't think he was serious. He was pushing to see how far he could bend her to his will. She shook her head. "How could I? I've only been here a few months and know very little about the area."

He'd fixed her with a penetrating gaze, and she saw something else come into his mind that made her hold her breath.

"What I see is that no matter how much I want you, you don't want to work with me. Is it because I remind you of your ex-husband? Is he why you won't let me get near you?"

It took every ounce of her will to keep her eyes steady, not to blink or betray her shock.

"You do look like Ric, but that's only a physical resemblance. It's Bill Denton I see when I'm near you." She spoke with as much conviction as she could muster.

It seemed that minutes went by as he continued to search her eyes.

He sighed and let go of her hands. "So you won't go," he said quietly.

"I can't." Her voice was just as quiet.

He turned to the door. "Thank you for coming over," he said.

"I enjoyed the pie," she said stiffly, her chin high as she followed him.

She couldn't leave him like that. She had to try one more time.

"There're so many other things you can do, Bill," she said, instinctively putting her hand on his arm. "You must do something for your own sake."

His face was expressionless as he opened the door for her.

"You run your life the way you see fit, and I'll run mine."

Chapter 27

Evelyn Hightower at the high school had been
delighted to hear that Bill would be available for the
photography program.

She introduced him to the group of twelve students
and urged them to pay attention. "This is the first time
we've been able to have this class, so it's important that
you make it work so we can have it again."

Bill called names from the roll sheet of the seven
boys and five girls, including Lynn, Ross, and Keisha.
There were a few other kids he knew while the others
were total strangers to him. No matter. If he did his job
right, they'd all be friends at the end of the six weeks,
exchanging ideas and learning from each other.

"Why do you want to take pictures?" he asked.

"I want to make a good family album."

"Not me, I like taking pictures of buildings."

"I'm interested in animals."

"I like sports."

"Any outdoor stuff."

"Whatever moves, like cars, trucks, boats."

These were the same kinds of answers he usually got
to this question, but he noticed that two of the twelve
hadn't answered. Both were boys. When he repeated it

to them, one said, "I see something, but I don't know if the camera sees the same thing." Maybe a budding photographer, Bill thought.

The other boy shrugged. "Don't know. It's just something different to do."

At least he had an open mind, and who knew—that something different might become a lasting interest.

"Since this is a short course, you weren't required to have a certain kind of camera. Let's see what you brought with you."

As he suspected, most had an inexpensive drugstore type, and he sighed at the challenge of teaching them anything except how to get the best image these cameras could produce.

If even one student was inspired enough to move on to a better camera, he'd be satisfied. Meanwhile, knowing the impatience of teens, he quickly gave them some fundamental concepts beginning with the Ansel Adams one that guided his work: "Forget what it looks like. How does it feel?"

The resulting questions and lively discussion made the hour go fast.

"Next week I'll give you an assignment," he announced as the bell rang. They left talking excitedly among themselves.

He felt better than he had in a long time. Deciding what kind of assignments to give to this youthful, inexperienced group with wide interests was a task to challenge his imagination. And that quiet boy—what was his name, Mark?—was one to keep an eye on because already he saw the camera as more than an electronic toy.

He was in his office sketching out plans for the course when he answered the door to let Dan in.

"Haven't seen you since you made that Kahlua cake for me, Bill," Dan said. "Thought I'd come by and thank you in person." He looked around the kitchen. "Don't guess you've got any stashed away, have you?"

"Nope. Got some pecan brownies, though. Want some?" He filled the coffee pot, glad Dan had dropped by.

"Have I ever said no to your food?" Dan made himself comfortable at the table. "Been telling you for years you ought to have a sideline. Don't give up photography, but sell your food as well, especially your baking. You'd make lots of money." He took a brownie from the plate Bill put on the table and ate it in two bites.

Bill poured the coffee and passed a mug to Dan. "Have some coffee with your next two bites." Amusement crinkled his eyes.

"I'm not proud," Dan said and did exactly that. "If I passed these around at school, I'd get you more customers than you could handle. Seriously, Bro, have you ever thought of going professional with your cooking?"

"Not since college." He remembered giving that same answer to Nerissa when he was at her house on Christmas Eve. When they were friends. The thought made him wince inside.

"If you ever change your mind, let me know first. I'll be your sales rep." He inhaled another brownie and followed it with a swallow of coffee. "So what have you decided to do since the Nova Scotia thing flopped?" The concern in his eyes was apparent to Bill.

"Last month the high school asked me to do a six-week

photo club class. I said I had to wait to hear about Nova Scotia. I've heard, and I've all the time I need," he said grimly. He put a piece of brownie in his mouth. "Had the first session today."

"Going to be any good?"

"I'll do what I can with twelve kids. Most probably don't have a lasting interest in it, but at least they'll know more about photography than they did before."

"Teach them how to avoid chopping off heads of tall people in their pictures," Dan advised. "I've lost my head more times than I can count."

"I'll do that." Bill filled Dan's mug without asking.

"That class is only temporary. What else will you do?"

He saw Dan was back to being serious, but having no ready answer he shrugged his shoulders and sipped his coffee as he stared out the window.

"What'd your lady say about it?" Dan asked quietly.

"My lady?" he repeated, raising an eyebrow.

Dan continued to look at him, waiting for an answer.

He shouldn't have been surprised considering how Dan had kept up with his relationship with Nerissa, if you could call it that. He didn't want to talk about it, but he knew from experience how hard it was to put Dan off. He could be very persistent. It wasn't from nosiness, though, it was because he cared. So he might as well try to pull his thoughts together.

"She thinks I ought to go anyway since I've put so much time into it."

He threw the words out as if they meant little to him.

"You tell her yes or no?" Dan turned his mug as if the answer was in there.

"I told her I'd go if she went with me." Just saying the words still stung.

Dan looked up and Bill saw not only surprise but approval in his glance. "Go on. I'm listening."

Bill couldn't sit still as he recounted the conversation. He went over to the stove. "It was a solid idea and we could work together, me doing the camera part and her doing the writing." He lifted a pan from the stove and put it on the counter. "She said it'd be a great adventure, but she couldn't go."

He opened the refrigerator, took out a package of meat, and slammed it into the sink. "I asked why not, and she kept saying she had a business to run." He came to rest against the wall and ran his fingers through his hair. " 'So do I,' I said, 'but we wouldn't have to be gone that long. We could make it happen if we wanted to do it together.' "

He sat down again and dropped his head in his hands. "I've never been so near begging a woman as I did her. She still said no."

He'd tried over and over to tell himself it didn't really matter, but it was like an aching tooth that he couldn't keep from biting down on.

He was afraid he'd see pity in Dan's eyes, but when he raised his head, what he saw was understanding and speculation.

"You don't have to worry that she said no because she doesn't care for you, Bro," Dan said.

"She's got a funny way of showing it," he muttered, then looked at Dan hopefully. "What makes you think she does?"

"I've seen the way she looks at you. I've seen the way

you two are together. When you didn't tell her you were part of DB, she wasn't just angry. She was hurt because her feelings were already involved. So there has to be another reason she won't go to Nova Scotia with you," he mused.

Bill watched Dan, thinking he hadn't mentioned how he'd confronted her about her ex-husband. That was too near the bone. He'd come up against a barrier he couldn't move. And although she denied it, he was certain her marriage was involved. If she didn't care for him enough, despite the connection he knew was there, what could he do? He couldn't force her to confide in him.

The problem was, this was new territory for him and he didn't know the terrain. He'd never experienced such complex emotions for a woman, never felt an attraction that grew stronger each time he was with her, involved a clash of wills, and tested him as a man.

He came out of his thoughts to meet Dan's keen gaze. "I remember asking you once before if you were going to walk away from this like you have others."

"I can't." The circumstances were different now, and more was at stake than when Dan first asked. But his heart gave him the truth.

"Good," was Dan's forceful response. "On that you can pour me another coffee and I'll have a brownie."

When he served them both again, Bill asked, "Were you worried about my answer?"

"Yeah, because that's what I did. Of course, Jenny and I were already married and we'd had the usual little blow-ups that we could put right with a little honest talking and lovemaking. After a while, as little arguments grew into big ones that didn't work. Things went from bad to worse and we grew apart. Then she asked for a divorce. Let me tell you, Bro, that was the worse move your stupid big brother ever made." He shook his head in rueful disbelief.

"Getting the divorce?" He'd never heard Dan speak so intimately about the breakup of his marriage.

Dan nodded emphatically. "I should've said, 'No divorce. Let's see if we can patch this up,' but macho man like me, I couldn't bring myself to do that. I was angry, frustrated, and nursing hurt pride and ego. I loved her, but I let that get buried under the other stuff." He looked out into space as if seeing that younger Dan.

I'm the guy who took all those courses in psychology so I could understand people and take better pictures, Bill thought, *yet here's my brother I'm close to and I didn't know how he felt about Jenny. He acted like a cool, in-charge man and that's what I saw.*

Dan fixed him with a piercing eye. "I'm telling you this, Bro, so you won't be that way. You'll be sorry forever."

"I hear you," he acknowledged. "Do you ever see Jenny?" Now that he saw beneath the surface, he hoped there was still a chance for Dan and Jenny since neither had remarried.

The lines around Dan's mouth softened. "We've been talking on the phone, and I think she's going to let me visit her pretty soon.

"This is just between you and me," he warned as he got up from the table. "For heaven's sake, don't tell Mom."

As Bill stepped outside with Dan, he automatically checked to see if the pickup was in the next driveway and was relieved to see it there. Worrying about

Nerissa's safety in the store was something he couldn't get rid of.

Dan backed out, blinked his lights, and drove away.

Was it because he was being a carbon copy of Dan that he'd pushed Nerissa away? It looked like she'd rejected him by saying she couldn't go just because he wanted her to.

Perhaps he needed to practice what he'd told the class today: Forget what it looks like. How does it feel?

It had been raining all day, and Nerissa felt as gray and gloomy as the weather. She sat in her office trying to consider the bookstore accounts.

The store was doing well. A few teachers had put in orders for the softcover books assigned in their classes. A group of senior ladies organized a book club to meet in one of the rooms weekly. The racks of black greeting cards were a good draw, and Sarah had turned out to be a jewel. She learned quickly and knew how to encourage customers not only to browse but to buy.

She should've been happy. Wasn't this what she'd been striving for? Her gaze lit on some misplaced titles, and she got to her feet to straighten them out. But happiness was far from what she was feeling since her argument with Bill. She found Rochelle Alers in H and put her back in A.

Her emotions were all over the place. She knew it was because what she felt for Bill was totally at war with her past experiences. The past made it difficult for her to trust Bill or herself.

What did he want with her besides going to Nova

Scotia? Was there something more for them? Or did he even know?

She moved to the second shelf. Gwynne Forster and Donna Hill were way over in the Ps. So easy to pick them up and put them in their proper place. But where was hers?

Could she release the fear that Bill might find she wasn't what he wanted after all and turn away as Ric had? She'd carried that baggage so long, and it was ruining her life. She needed to reclaim her life.

She looked back over the past few years. Somehow she'd found the strength and courage to make her dream of a bookstore a reality.

What was the reality that required that same strength and courage now? Putting the question like that made the answer blindingly simple. She was in love with Bill Denton.

Motionless, she stared at the book that she'd picked out of the Ws. *The Turning Point* by Francis Ray. Like an automaton, she put the book in the Rs and sat down to absorb the shock.

It was love, not just an attraction based on chemistry. Love was the invisible thread that had kept her responding to him all the way through, from gratitude and appreciation when he'd brought the gorgeous flowers to great resentment and disappointment when he'd not been with her at the bookstore opening.

She hadn't recognized it, but her heart knew it now. Sitting in her office, she experienced a blossoming of joy unlike anything she'd known.

If Bill walked in now, she wouldn't be able to hide it.

Then it struck her.

What would his reaction be?

She had to move again. She picked up a stack of new books that belonged in the history room and distributed them.

He felt something for her because he talked about the connection between them. He'd mentioned it just the last time they were together, then had kissed her in a way that made her want him to never stop. She leaned against the bookcase, closing her eyes, feeling the knot in the bottom of her stomach.

She didn't know what he meant by a connection, but she had to find out. For both of their sakes. If a nebulous connection and a sexual chemistry were what he felt, perhaps, like her, there was something much deeper that he just hadn't recognized.

Until he did, she had to restrain what she felt. Meanwhile, she had to figure out a way to get him talking to her again.

Chapter 28

Nerissa dialed Bill's number, not certain what she'd say when he answered. But she knew that the longer she waited to get in touch with him, the more difficult it would be.

"This is Denton's. Please leave your name and number and I'll get right back to you."

"Bill, this is Nerissa at the bookstore." Maybe it was better this way. "Please call me about some pictures I need to have taken. Thanks."

Since it was a job, hopefully he'd come. If not, she'd think of some other way to talk to him. She was in the storeroom checking inventory an hour later when Sarah buzzed her. "Phone's for you."

"This is Nerissa," she said.

"This is Bill, returning your call."

He sounded cautious, but she couldn't be sure and it didn't matter. He'd called her back!

"Hey, Bill. I wonder if I could see you here at the bookstore to talk about pictures of the store for a magazine article. Any time you can make it is okay with me." She stopped and held her breath. Would he come or make an excuse? Thirty seconds that seemed like an hour passed.

Then she heard him say, "I happen to be free right now."

"Wonderful." She released her breath. "Please come."

In the bathroom, she combed her hair again and freshened her lipstick. Her eyes were sparkling like stars. She blinked a few times, but the anticipation of seeing Bill still made them shine.

She'd decided against letting him see how she felt. It wouldn't be wise to embarrass him with an unwanted show of affection that he might not be able to return. Still, excitement filled her as she returned to her office and sat down at the computer.

The door opened and Bill came in.

She wasn't aware of moving, yet she was standing on her side of the counter, clutching it so she wouldn't give in to her impulse to hold out her hands as he stood on the other side looking at her.

"Bill. How are you?" It was all she could get out as she drank him in—tall, handsome, and achingly familiar.

"Okay. How about you?" His dark eyes held hers inquiringly.

She had to do better than this or she'd stand there babbling like an idiot. "I'm fine. There's a bookstore magazine I'm going to send a story to, and it needs pictures. Would you be interested in taking them?"

"Of course. Show me what you have in mind." His gaze followed her as she came around the counter.

"Let's look at each room and we can talk about the kind of activity it hosts."

She introduced him to Sarah, who was working in the young readers' room.

"When do you get the most kids in here?" Bill asked.

"On Saturdays, when their parents can bring them," she said.

"Usually in the afternoon," Sarah added.

At the door to the fiction room, Nerissa accidentally brushed against him and felt electricity rush through her. She looked up to see his eyes fixed on her. In the other rooms, although they talked about the types and number of pictures her story needed, the tension rose steadily, and by the time they came to the kitchen, with its table and chairs, she was very nervous.

"Please have a chair, Bill," she said as she sat across from him. "A book club meets in here and we've had another group ask about it. But as you can see, it's pretty small." She glanced everywhere but at him.

She clenched her hands in her lap and made herself look directly into his eyes.

"Bill, I want to apologize for what I said to you. I'd no business telling you what to do. Will you forgive me?"

The corners of his mouth turned up and the contours of his sober face changed. "I was wrong too. Can we forgive each other and go on from there?"

"Yes, please." Instinctively she reached for his hand to find he was doing the same. His touch and the steady warmth of his gaze flowing over her made her forget everything except him. For the first time, she had the desire to tell him about Ric Cooper, and she knew this was the time to do it.

"I want to tell you about my marriage, Bill," she said.

He leaned across the table and put out his other hand for hers, then held them firmly. "I've been needing to know," he said with a penetrating gaze.

"I told you the night you came to the bookstore that

Ric and I both worked for the library. I was a different person than I am now. I was younger and believed in people and that when you got married, your vows meant something. Ric said he believed in the same things and that he wanted children, as I did."

She paused. This was harder than she'd thought it would be, but she had to do it. His eyes encouraged her, his hands gave her security.

"Go on," he murmured.

"I thought we were happy the first year. I was promoted to head librarian. They gave me a party, but Ric couldn't make it. He was away. We had more income and I thought we could afford to start our family. But he said to wait a little, he wasn't ready. Ric liked to go to restaurants and parties that to me were overpriced and loud. He thought it was important to be seen. If I protested, he thought I was being domineering and bossy. Still, there were times when we got along, so I kept hoping the marriage would get better."

She'd been looking at their hands on the table and she came to a stop. This was the most difficult part because it was humiliating.

Bill said her name. "Nerissa."

When she looked up, he said, "You're coming to the hardest part. Right?"

She nodded.

"Be the Nerissa I know. Put your shoulders back, tilt your chin, and let those green eyes blaze while you tell me what that creep did to you!"

"He was away or he made excuses so that we rarely slept together. Then one day a pretty young graduate student who was obviously pregnant came to see me. She said she was six months pregnant with Ric's child, and she begged me to divorce him so they could marry for the baby's sake. That same day I had the locks changed, put his belongings outside, and filed for a divorce."

Her shoulders were still back and her chin was high, but she felt a glaze of tears in her eyes.

The next thing she knew, he had her up from the chair and was pressing her head on his chest.

"Don't cry, baby. He wasn't worth it," he said, stroking her hair.

But it wasn't Ric she was crying for. It was those wasted years of her youth, her unborn children, all mixed up with the solid relief of finding she could trust Bill with her story and that she had the courage to destroy that barrier between them.

The phone buzzed. She swallowed hard and answered it.

"Sorry to bother you, Nerissa, but it's the high school about Lynn," Sarah said.

"This is Nerissa Ramsey."

"Miss Ramsey, there's a problem with your niece, and the principal would like you to come to his office right away."

"What's happened? Is Lynn all right?" She felt Bill's arm supporting her.

"She's all right. She and another student were in the coach's room, where they had no right to be. They were apparently trying to take a picture of one of the trophies and broke it. Shall I tell Principal Rupert you're on your way?"

"I'm leaving right now."

"What's the problem?" Bill asked anxiously.

"Lynn and someone else tried to take a picture of a trophy and broke it. They were in the coach's office, where they shouldn't have been." She looked at him speculatively. "The other person was probably Ross."

"They must have been working on my assignment from yesterday to take a picture of something that's beautiful to you, but why couldn't they use common sense?" He watched as she went to the sink and dabbed cold water on her eyes.

"What will they do to them?" Her eyes still felt uncomfortable from her crying, so she washed them again.

"Other than replace the trophy, I don't know." He handed her his clean handkerchief.

"The reason my sister sent Lynn here is because she almost got suspended for something that wasn't her fault. But this is. Do you think they'll suspend her?" She couldn't keep the apprehension out of her voice as she looked up at him.

He placed his hands on either side of her face. "Your eyes look better." He kissed each one gently. "Don't worry about Lynn being suspended, baby. We'll work it out. I'll follow you there."

Twenty minutes later, they were all gathered around the table in the conference room. She sat next to Lynn and Bill. Ross and his mother, Dee Russell, were there, as well as the principal, assistant principal, and the coach, Miss Markert.

She could see tearstains on Lynn's face, and Ross was red around the eyes. Observing them with the experienced eye of a school librarian, she was glad to see they looked chastened, not sullen. She'd only met the principal twice, and although she seemed formal, she sensed she'd be hard but fair. Bill had turned out to be on a first-name basis with everyone in the room, and she hoped fervently that would help.

When asked by the principal, Lynn, with an apologetic look at Bill, said they had been searching for something beautiful to photograph. Remembering the crystal trophy with the sun shining on it, she and Ross had gone to the coach's office. The door wasn't locked, so they went in. Ross took the trophy down from the shelf. Lynn said she was trying to move it so it would catch the light, and it slipped from her hands. They tried to catch it, but it fell and shattered on the floor.

Lynn burst into tears again. "I'm so sorry, Coach," she said, turning to Miss Markert. "I didn't mean any harm."

"I know you didn't, but that's the problem, isn't it? My trophy's gone because you and Ross didn't think. You just went ahead with what you wanted to do. The door was closed, which means stay out. I shouldn't have to lock my door every time I go out." She flung her shoulder-length hair impatiently.

The principal gave Ross a chance to speak, Mrs. Hightower summarized Lynn's and Ross's grades and records, and Bill spoke about the assignment and their participation in his class. Then the principal told Lynn and Ross to stand.

"This is a serious matter," she said soberly. "What's involved here is trespassing and breakage of personal property. But you had no criminal intent. What you had was poor judgment in carrying out a legitimate class assignment. You and your parents or guardians will have to replace the trophy, and you have to leave Mr. Denton's class."

After the conference, Nerissa and Dee Russell, a compact, no-nonsense woman, spoke with the coach, who said she'd get them a photo of her trophy and the name of the company that made it.

When they were in the parking lot, Dee took Nerissa aside. "Ross's dad is going to be real mad at Ross about this, Nerissa. What're you going to do about Lynn?"

"Ground her for a month, that's first. Then find some way for her to earn money for the trophy. Maybe this'll teach her not to follow every impulse she gets." As Dee still looked worried, she said, "They're not bad kids, Dee. Ross's dad knows that."

"We all know it, and that's the only thing that makes this easier to get through." She took her keys out, collected Ross, and left.

An hour ago she was confiding in Bill about her disastrous marriage, Nerissa thought as she walked over to her pickup, where he and Lynn were talking. But they didn't finish, and now there was Lynn to deal with.

Bill put his arm around her shoulder. She was so thankful for his nearness, she didn't care that Lynn saw the gesture.

"How are you?" he wanted to know.

The concern in his eyes raised her spirits. "I'm okay," she said.

"You going home or back to the store?"

"It's not closing time yet, so I'll go to the store."

"Do you need me to go with you or shall I drop Lynn home?" They both glanced at the silent girl sitting in the pickup.

"She'd better go with me, but thanks."

"Nerissa, I know you're concerned about her right

now, but don't forget about us. We have a conversation to finish, so call me as soon as you can. I'll be waiting."

His eyes held a promise that sustained her through conversations with Lynn and later with Alice and Greg, before and after they'd talked with Lynn.

"They were very severe with her," she told Bill later that night on the phone. She'd showered and was in bed, thankful the evening was over.

"Because this is her second time to mess up?" he asked.

"Right, and I think she's truly scared now. She said she doesn't want to go through the rest of her high school years getting in trouble. She and I are going to do some reading about adolescence. It might help her. Anyway, it'll give her something to do while she's grounded."

"Lynn has my sympathy, but I want to know when I can see you, Nerissa." His voice caressed her name. "Come over tomorrow evening. Please." His invitation held a promise that made her shiver as she agreed.

Chapter 29

Nerissa had been in turmoil all day.

At six a.m., Lynn, suddenly realizing that at school that day she'd have to face embarrassment and snickers, decided she wasn't going. Nerissa gave her a stern lecture on the consequences of one's actions and advised her that by bus or her pickup, school was on her agenda every day, and she'd live through it.

At work a shipment of books still hadn't been delivered, and she'd spent an hour tracking them.

Her evening with Bill loomed ahead, and each time she thought of it some question arose.

Yesterday he'd been wonderful, standing by her at the school. His unquestioning support had opened her eyes. If this was a part of his true colors, then the future, if they had one, looked great.

But what about children? Did he like them? Did it matter that she was five years older than he? Did her story about her marriage make her seem pathetic? Did he think she was one of those domineering women just because she spoke her mind? Perhaps she wasn't soft and feminine enough for him.

As she walked up his steps that evening, she felt like a leaf that had been wind-tossed all day. He must have been watching for her because he had the door open by the time she reached it.

He took her coat, and in the soft light of the lamps scrutinized her face.

"You're nervous," he said softly.

"A little," she said, tugging at her blouse.

"So am I," he admitted and, to her surprise, flushed.

He led her to the couch. "If we sit together, we can help each other get over it."

He plumped up the pillows behind her and offered her juice, water or coffee, all of which she refused. The nervousness she'd never seen before in him had a calming effect on her. He was feeling the way she had yesterday at the table before she told him about Ric and their marriage.

"Before anything else, Nerissa, thank you for telling me about Ric. It's been driving me crazy ever since Lynn said I was so much like him. I figured that everything I did that you didn't like was like something he did. But you wouldn't tell me about him, so it was like fighting a ghost. That's partly true, isn't it? You've got to be honest with me."

He sat forward on the couch, his hands clasped tightly, and stared intently into her eyes.

"You're right. That was partly true." She stared back, her hands relaxed in her lap.

"I know the main part. It was when he didn't show for your promotion party and I didn't show for your opening. That's right, isn't it?"

He scarcely waited for her assent but plowed on, his voice rising.

"The big difference is that I wanted to be there, had

every intention of being there, and tried my best to be there." He took a deep breath, then shook his head.

"The point is, I wasn't there on your big day and it's been killing me. Will you forgive me?" His eyes appealed for her understanding.

"I do, Bill. Truly. Don't worry about it anymore." She'd no idea he felt deeply about that day. She'd assumed he'd forgotten it after telling her what happened. Another misjudgment on her part.

He still didn't seem reassured. Following her instinct, she scooted forward, put her arms around him, and kissed him. It was like opening a floodgate. Her love poured into her embrace, igniting a spark between them.

Bill crushed her to him and returned the kiss again and again. When they were both breathless, he raised his head. He tried to speak but had to swallow.

Her heart was beating so hard, she could scarcely feel anything else and she was mesmerized by his fervent gaze.

"Listen to me while I still have my sanity, sweetheart," he said. "I love you. I'm crazy about you. Will you marry me, Nerissa? Will you be my beautiful green-eyed wife and the mother of my children?"

The world stood still as his words echoed in her heart.

"Oh, yes, Bill, yes, yes." She felt like she was singing but she couldn't help herself.

He was still, waiting, until she said, "I love you, Bill, with all my heart and soul." She felt the tension leave his body as he gathered her up, raining soft kisses on her eyes, her cheeks, the tip of her nose and her mouth. His whispered endearments and tender caresses made her feel beautiful, although no one had ever called her that until now.

"Every woman wants to be called beautiful, even when her mirror tells her something else," she said dreamily. "I was afraid of being too plain for you."

His eyes bored into her. "Plain? That so-and-so did a job on you, baby. But I'm going to turn it around. Why do you think you were the center of attention at the party? Why do you think my heart jumps when I look at you? You're a beautiful woman, inside and out."

The admiration in his eyes made her tingle, but before she could muster a reply, he went on. "What I want to know now is how many?" His hands stroked her back up and down, sending tremors through her.

"How many what?" She let her fingers graze the firm, warm skin of his neck and felt him shiver.

"How many children do you want?"

She grew still. Here was her secret fear but she had to face it, lay it in the open for him to see. She straightened her shoulders, tilted her chin, and narrowed her direct gaze. "I'm thirty-nine, Bill, older than you, and maybe too old to give you children."

Now she had to wait for his response.

He studied her, his gaze deepening its intensity and causing an agitation along her nerves. If what she said bothered him, better to know it now because her age wasn't something that could be changed.

"I don't care how old you are, Nerissa." He held her by the shoulders. "It's you I love whatever age you are. I love the way you take me on without backing down because I'm a man. You're a woman with principle, you're smart and determined. You're a strong woman, but a woman who can melt in my arms." His voice was husky as he caught her against him and kissed her, demanding a response.

It came from unsuspected depths, fueled by the passion she no longer needed to restrain. When his tongue pressed against her mouth, she opened to let him in. Wave after wave of sensations engulfed her until their mutual caresses left her weak and trembling.

In an effort to regain her equilibrium, she laid her palms against his chest and tried to cool down by fanning herself with her hand. "I think the question was how many children," she said. "Why don't we start with one and see how it goes?"

"Makes sense to me." He skimmed his hand over her hair. "So when do you want to get married? Next week?" When her eyes widened he said, "Too soon? How about week after next?"

She hadn't thought that far ahead, and she knew it showed in her expression. "Four weeks is too short a time," she protested.

"How long do you need? After all, we have to get started on our family."

Although he kept a straight face, the heat in his eyes, the underlying seriousness in his voice, and the instant response in her stomach made her blush. Reminding herself that he said he liked her directness, she said, "I feel the same way." The electricity flashed between them, and she hurried on. "However, since I'm going to marry one of the most eligible bachelors in town, I intend to do it in high style!" She winked at him. "Seriously, our families would be hurt if we rushed it."

"You're right," he acknowledged, "and we've got two houses and Lynn to think about, too."

"Would you like to reconsider this proposition, Mr. Denton?" She faced him, shoulders back, chin out, and looked him in the eye. This time she wore a big, happy smile and her green eyes were sparkling.

"No way. This time I'm getting not only a tenant for life, but a partner, a friend, a lover, and a wife!"

He pulled her into his arms, and this time his kisses told her that she was loved and that she was secure, protected, and cherished.

Epilogue

They'd worked it out. Nerissa's house had been rented to a family with two college-age children. Bill had moved his studio to downtown Jamison, thus making room for Lynn, who'd returned to Seattle at the end of the school year.

Bill knew he'd never been so happy when Nerissa, on the arm of her father, had walked down the aisle toward him that first Saturday in April. She was everything and more than he'd ever hoped for. That night, when he made love to her for the first time, he'd whispered, "I adore you!"

Now the Book Boutique was overflowing on this Sunday afternoon in June. He and Nerissa were autographing their second book, *Our Low Country*, with photographs by William Denton and essays by Nerissa Ramsey Denton.

They'd written the first one after their honeymoon three years ago in Nova Scotia. As he'd foretold, their collaboration produced great work. The critical praise the book had garnered brought them several offers.

The offers were presently shelved while Nerissa stayed home to care for one-year-old William George Denton and enjoy her second pregnancy.

He looked at her now as she settled a sleepy Billy in her arms. She was radiant, and there was a softness in her eyes that hadn't been there before.

She rubbed her stomach. "What?" he asked.

"Our daughter just kicked me," she said, laying her hand on his arm.

He covered it with his. "I adore you," he said for her ears alone.

Once, he'd thought she was not in his future, but the gods had ruled otherwise. She'd filled the empty spaces he hadn't even known existed. Now, with her at his side, he was secure, loved, and cherished.

Dear Readers,

Writing is revelation, as you know. In *Change of Heart*, my first book, Emily Brooks was the initial heroine who came to my mind. She was gentle, reserved, and modest.

In the seven books that have followed, heroines with other characteristics have been explored as they were revealed to my writer's imagination.

As you read *Cherished,* you'll see that Nerissa Ramsey is a far cry from Emily Brooks. Yet each woman strives, through dealing with her own strengths and weaknesses, to find her way to fulfillment.

Isn't that what life is about for each of us? I'd love to hear your comments and thanks for reading my books.

Please write to me and I'll reply.

Adrienne Ellis Reeves
P.O. Box 9035
Moreno Valley, CA 92552

ABOUT THE AUTHOR

Adrienne Ellis Reeves, a native of Illinois, earned her BA and MA at San Jose State University in San Jose, California. She received her Ed.D. at the University of Massachusetts at Amherst. She has traveled extensively throughout the United States, Canada and Bermuda in the interests of the Baha'i Faith. This interest took her and her late husband, William, to Summerville, South Carolina, upon her retirement. Their three children, six grandchildren, and one great-grandchild reside in California and New York.

Dr. Reeves's writing career began with magazine articles and a children's book, *Willie and the Number Three Door.* These were followed by a series of novels and novellas set in the fictional town of Jamison, South Carolina. They are a part of the permanent South Caroliniana collection at the University of South Carolina in Columbia.

After twenty-five years, Dr. Reeves is returning to California, but she intends to continue writing about the South Carolina Lowcountry that she loves.